COMFORT ME WITH APPLES

COMFORT ME WITH APPLES

SARA O'LEARY

THISTLEDOWN PRESS

Canadian Cataloguing in Publication Data

O'Leary, Sara.

Comfort me with apples

ISBN 1-895449-81-2

1. Title.
PS8579.L293 C65 1998   C813'.54   C98-920173-2
PR 9199.3.0385 C65 1998

Book and cover design by J. Forrie
Art Direction A.M. Forrie
Typeset by Thistledown Press Ltd.
Cover painting: *Woman Walking With Orange*
by Christine Lynn

Printed and bound in Canada by
Veilleux Impression à Demande
Boucherville, Quebec

Thistledown Press Ltd.
633 Main Street
Saskatoon, Saskatchewan
S7H 0J8

**Saskatchewan
Arts Board**

THE CANADA COUNCIL | LE CONSEIL DES ARTS
FOR THE ARTS | DU CANADA
SINCE 1957 | DEPUIS 1957

Thistledown Press gratefully acknowledges the financial assistance of the Canada
Council for the Arts, the Saskatchewan Arts Board, and the Government of
Canada through the Book Publishing Industry Development Program for its
publishing program.

CONTENTS

ACKNOWLEDGEMENTS

Love and gratitude to Daniel and Liam.

Many thanks to Seán Virgo for his intelligent and intuitive editing assistance.

Some of these stories have appeared in *Coming Attractions* (Oberon, 1990), *Grain, The New Quarterly, The Moosehead Anthology* and *Matrix*. The author is grateful for assistance received from the Saskatchewan Arts Board and the Canada Council.

Dedicated, with love, to my mother for understanding that all mothers depicted here are completely fictional, and any resemblance to any real mothers, living or dead, is purely coincidental.

Comfort me with apples, for I am sick of love.

— *Song of Songs*

No one can write about perfect love because it cannot be committed to words even by those who know about it.

— *Ethel Wilson,* Swamp Angel

THE SUMMER HOUSE

1. *I Wish I May, I Wish I Might*

The five of us moved into the house we'd rented for the summer on the first day of May. I hadn't lived in a house since I left home. We were already calling the house our summer place, but it was hard to believe it was summer since it still got so cold at night. Still, it was a nice cold with the house so near and warm. I had made a brief escape into the backyard with the bottle of Southern Comfort. I knew that even if they didn't come looking for me they'd surely come looking for the bottle.

There was a yellow light spilling out of the back window, and from where I was standing I could see through the dining room and into the living room. Just outside my line of vision Nigel was playing his guitar and Lucy was singing along, off-key and too loud, as usual. I listened for the song to end and Lucy's laughter to bubble over.

It was dark in the yard and I knew that even if any of them happened to look in my direction they wouldn't be able to see me, and so I stood, invisible, at the window and watched them. Maeve was all folded up into the armchair, her feet tucked beneath her and her hands curled up inside her sleeves.

She looked like she was trying to pull some sort of disappearing act. She was watching Lucy sing, and I watched her watching. Will was on the floor, slinking around to surprise Maeve from behind. For a second I thought of rapping on the glass to warn her, but then his arms came up from behind the chair and his hands closed over her eyes. Maeve laughed and reached up. Taking one of Will's hands she planted a kiss in his palm.

I backed away from the window then and into the yard. Earlier in the day we had strung up a hammock between the two big trees, and then we all stood around waiting to see who would be the first to try it. I laid myself down in the hammock, carefully, waiting for the crash. It didn't come and I slowly felt all the tensed muscles in my body let go. I took a long pull from the bottle and leaned back to look up at the sky. Just as I looked up I saw a falling star, a shooter.

The summer before I'd been up at the lake and had spent more time watching the skies than ever before in my life. I saw the northern lights, a meteorite shower, and had all the constellations suddenly mapped out for me. But this star was my own, part of my sky. It happened so fast that I forgot to make a wish. What do you want? I don't know . . . nothing really . . . to be happy, I suppose . . . whatever that means.

2. happy families are all alike

Will calls us the post-nuclear family. We are what we have left. We are closer than family, he says, because we chose each other.

I never had a sister, although I always wanted one and used to pester and petition my mother for one. *Please, please,*

please Mom. But for some reason my parents had me and that was it. I'm not even sure that I was on purpose.

I met Lucy in the bar one night after going to see a show she was in that Nigel was running lights for. That was back when he and I were a couple, of sorts. I thought she was trying to pick me up. The music was really loud, one of those half-hearted guitar players with an over-enthusiastic rhythm box and I couldn't tell if she said: I can tell we're going to get along, or, I can tell we're going to get it on. Either way she was holding my hand, which made me nervous. I'm not a touchy-feely person.

Lucy is Lucy and there's nobody else in the world like her. She's the sister that God was holding out on me. On rainy nights she comes to sleep in my bed with me, steals all the pillows, makes herself comfortable and then says: *tell me a story.* So I do. She'll say: *stroke my hair.* And because it's Lucy, I do.

3. mid-life with flowers

"Will is turning thirty," said Maeve.

"Not a damn thing we can do about it," said Nigel.

"We could throw him a party," Lucy said. "A surprise party. I've always wanted to have a surprise party. They look like such fun on TV."

We were playing bridge — Nigel was teaching us how — and Lucy was the dummy. Typecasting.

"It's for Will, not you," I reminded her.

"Well," said Lucy, looking like a chastened child and then slowly beginning to beam again. "You don't have to tell me who's coming."

The night of the party Will was working until ten. He asked us to come down and meet him at the bar when he got off, and we could have those drinks that you set on fire. We all made vague maybe-noises and then, once he left, we clapped our hands at our own cleverness.

By a quarter of nine we had the whole house set up. Lucy had baked a chocolate layer cake that had a definite tilt to it. She solved the problem by making up an extra batch of icing and building up the fallen side. Nigel told her she would have made an excellent engineer. Lucy said she'd rather be the guy who rides in the caboose and waves at little kids. Sometimes I wonder what it would be like to be Lucy.

People started arriving at nine and Lucy went upstairs to hide as soon as she heard the doorbell. "Don't tell me who it is," she said. "I don't want to spoil the surprise."

By eleven that night some thirty of us had been sardined into Lucy's bedroom for close to an hour and a half. Every late arrival would send us crouching, shushing our nearest neighbour into silence. *Shh, shh, it's Will.* Only it never was. By about ten-thirty we'd grown tired of turning the light on and off (Franz described it as a geriatric strobe) and had settled for the dark. I really enjoyed sitting in the dark with my very best friends and about a dozen near-strangers. There was something perversely intimate about the fact that every time you shifted you were likely to brush one of your limbs against some invisible other's limbs. *I wish all parties could be like this,* I thought.

Will got home at midnight, drunk and sloppy as only a drunken Will can be. We didn't even hear him come in. By this time the party had broken out of the bedroom and was going full blast. Nigel was playing guitar — a Patsy Cline song I think — and he stopped in the middle of a line when he saw Will standing in the middle of the room.

"You don't love me," Will said. "Any of you."

Will drunk is prone to melodrama and Bette Davis delivery. You can always tell when Bette's surfacing because Will lights a cigarette. Will doesn't smoke and even drunk he only uses the cigarette as a prop to punctuate his sentences with.

"You're nothing but false friends, all of you." Will made a sweeping gesture with one arm and then fell back into the armchair, covering his face with his hands.

You'd think he'd have to be pretty blind drunk not to notice the streamers, the balloons, the cake, the wine glasses, the pyramid of gifts, the bevy of friends with, now, fallen faces.

Lucy was standing in front of him holding a lit sparkler in each hand, staring at them, watching them flicker and burn as though she were bewitched. Nigel put down his guitar and went out into the kitchen — probably to wait until the scene was over. I couldn't think what to do. Maeve was the one to finally make a move; she walked over to Will and sat down on the arm of his chair, leaning over him so her hair would tickle his face.

"Will," she said. "We're sorry." She said it with that funny crack her voice sometimes has.

Will took his hands down and his face was a huge Puckish grin.

"Surprise," he said.

4. the shut-in

Some nights everyone will make plans to go off somewhere, out dancing or whatever, and at the last minute I'll decide to stay home. Tonight is one of those times.

"C'mon, don't be such a Biddie McGillicutty."

Mrs. McGillicutty is our neighbour across the way who we've never met. Actually we've never even seen her. She never leaves the house except in the middle of the night when there's nobody about. The only way we know that she's been out at all is that there'll be some new oddity in her yard: shiny red balls on the trees, copper bottom pots nailed to the side of her shed, most often just another layer of cardboard, plastic or plywood on top of the multiple layers already covering the windows and doorways to her house. We're not even sure how she can get out. I don't think Mrs. McGillicutty is her real name. Will made it up one night after I yelled at him to stop calling her "that crazy old broad."

The nights that I can persuade everybody to go dancing without me are a perverse luxury. The house, emptied of inhabitants, has a pulse all its own. Floors creak, the fridge hums and clicks off, tree branches drag their fingernails across window panes.

Once they've all changed their clothes four times, had a drink and picked a place to go, called friends and waited for them to call back, determined whether there's enough money to put gas in Will's car, and poured themselves out the front door, I am ready to collapse with relief like an anxious house-wife on a school morning.

When the house is empty I play Goldilocks and move from bedroom to bedroom: lying down in the beds, primping in the mirrors, looking out the windows for new views.

After only an hour of this, the silence begins to take on weight. I begin to crave the ringing of a phone or the slamming of a door. I start to wonder where they've gone, and if they are dancing at Ezzie's or drinking draught at the Drawing Room, or if they've gone to Kentucky Fried Chicken or maybe the donut place, only it isn't late enough yet. It takes about two hours for me to get angry. Why didn't they take me? Okay, I said I didn't want to go, but did they argue hard enough? Why didn't they try to persuade me? Why am I left all alone?

I'd like to know what Biddie McGillicutty does in her house all day and all night with no one to talk to. She must have a story: a one true love who went off to war never to return, a reprobate husband who drank up the family fortune and ran away with the false best friend, parents who disowned the wild and wilful daughter, children who moved to Australia and never call. What would she do, I wonder, if I were to knock on her door and say: *can I interest you in a cup of tea?*

By the time everybody comes home, drunk and smelling of sweat and smoke, danced out and weary, laughing at an obscure joke that never comes out right in the explaining and ends with *I guess you had to be there,* by that time I've missed them too long to be grateful for their too-real presence. By that time I know I'll never explain to them how the Christmas angel got on top of the fir tree in Mrs. McGillicutty's backyard.

5. *the forest*

Maeve is a little bit in love with Will. We all are I guess. Will's the type that nobody's immune to. He gets cruised by girls all the time and doesn't know what to do about it. *Do I have to wear a sign?* he asks. *Do I have to go up to people and say: Hello, I'm Will and I'm gay?*

There was a time when I thought I was in love with Will, but then I thought better of it. Now he's just the brother I never had and I try not to think incestuous thoughts.

Maeve can't stand it when Will flounces about and plays the queen, making the rest of us weak with laughter. This is why I think it's a bad thing for Maeve to be in love with Will. *He is what he is*, I told her. Maeve didn't say anything, just sucked on her lower lip like she always does when she doesn't want to talk about something.

A girl has been calling the house all week asking for Will. He says she was in the bar one night when he was working. Like the rest of us, Will loves a good dilemma and is playing this one for all it's worth. "Not only is she barking up the wrong tree," says Will, "she's not even in the right forest."

6. *diaper pails*

Are we still young? we wonder. We are all reaching and passing the ages our mothers were when they gave birth to us. This year my mother is exactly double my age and I am exactly one half hers. I know that she sometimes looks at me and sees herself and the choices that were made. I think that she sometimes envies me, but could she conceive of me envying her? It used to be that a family was what everyone had. The choices may have been limiting but at least they were clear cut.

Lucy asked her mother where she went to meet boys when she was her age and her mother said: *darling when I was your age, you were two.*

Our mothers were of the generation of the Beatles, we believe. We suspect them of smoking tea and dried banana peels and anything else that might do the trick. We picture them in tie-dye, and long hair with peace symbols on chains around their necks. But in the pictures they wear cashmere sweater sets, pearls, and June Allyson smiles.

Lucy's mother says she missed the sixties because she had her head in a diaper pail.

7. *coffee and sympathy*

Nigel was the only one still up when I got home from my date. I must have looked fairly wrecked because he offered to make me coffee without me even having to ask. By the time he came out of the kitchen with two cups of instant (the spoons still in the cups) and a handful of baby cookies, I was crying.

I hadn't meant to cry. It's something that I don't do very often and my lack of practice is evident. I make these horrid noises like a swimmer with a lung full of lake water. As a rule if I don't do a thing well I try to refrain from doing it at all.

Nigel hung back in the doorway, watching me, his expression moving from pity to fear to disgust and then through the gamut all over again. He looked down into the cups, back up at me, and then over his shoulder into the kitchen as though hoping someone was standing there waiting to relieve him. He took one step forward and two back and it was this awkwardness that finally saved me and I began to laugh.

At my laughter his face finally settled on an expression: court jester, willing to please. He curtsied deeply, spilling coffee on the rug in the process, and finally came over to me.

Nigel is a person who dreads physical intimacy. Sometimes when you touch him you can feel a physical withdrawal, a shudder. Nigel and I were lovers once, but that was all a long time ago and before we knew each other very well. What I mostly remember about that time was how mortified I was by the way he would get out of bed after making love and immediately put all his clothes back on.

"It can't be all that bad," he said, breaking a cookie and offering me half.

"Oh, it is though. It is."

"Did he do something horrible to you?" he asked.

"Who?" I asked. I'd forgotten how wonderful baby cookies can be when you're depressed.

"Your fellow, your gentleman caller, whoever it was that you were with."

"Oh, him. No. No, of course not. I don't even think he'd know how." I snuffled and sipped at my coffee, scalding my tongue with it.

"Well, what then?"

Why isn't Lucy up, I thought. She wouldn't make me feel silly or foolish for crying. She'd do things like offering me the sleeve of her bathrobe to wipe my nose on. Nigel was such a stick sometimes; even Will would have been better at offering comfort in his own self-centred way. Maeve would cry with me and that would either be worse or else it would actually make me feel better.

Nigel shifted beside me on the couch. He was probably trying to think of an excuse to get away.

"Do you want to talk about it?" he asked.

His asking, his willingness to listen, however reluctant, almost made me cry again. The worst thing someone can do when I'm falling apart is to be nice to me when I'm not expecting it. It makes me feel as though I've no skin to hold me together.

"No," I said. "I mean, yes, only I don't think . . . I don't know how to explain . . . it's just . . . nothing really . . . only . . . it's nothing really specific, I mean. Do you ever feel, or ever think that you're always . . . and it can happen at the silliest times like when somebody's going to kiss you goodnight, and they're moving toward you and your eyes are still open and you look at them and think . . . No this isn't how I mean to put it. Do you have any idea what I'm talking about?"

Nigel shook his head and gave me the last cookie.

"I guess what scares me," I said, "and it's silly and I shouldn't have cried, and it doesn't come from anywhere or anything that happened really, only do you ever think that you're always going to be alone?"

Nigel did a funny thing then. He didn't answer me, just stood up and set his coffee cup down on the table, took my empty cup out of my hands and set it down too, and then stood up and walked to the doorway. I thought he was just going to leave me there, that he couldn't hack any more of my hysteria. Instead he flicked the light switch and came back to sit beside me in the dark. He took my hand and just held it. That was all. I woke up a few hours later and he was still there, still holding my hand, and snoring gently.

8. bird legs

Maeve is willowy, slender, lithe — all those conjuring type words, but I'm just plain skinny. Words are funny things. Skinny doesn't even make any sense — it must come from *skin and bones*, but even the bones have been lost.

Skin. I remember one Thanksgiving — I would have been around four years old — watching my father carve the turkey. "Do you want a piece of the skin?" he asked, and I started to cry because I'd never thought of it quite like that. After that I nearly starved myself because I started thinking everything we ate was alive, or had been. I imagined carrots and potatoes having homes underground like gophers. A cake, rising in the oven, terrified me. I grew hysterical, feared nothing was safe to eat because it might suddenly come to life inside of me.

When I got older the kids at school called me bird legs and my mother would yell at me for wearing all my pairs of tights at once and making my legs sweat and chafe.

Then, when I was quite grown, nineteen maybe, I was taken to dinner at a French restaurant by a man who was a friend of my father's, which made it all very secret and forbidden. He ordered quail, which I had never had, and I don't know what I was expecting but when the waiter brought these little sparrow-like things I didn't know what to do. I stared at the man, my father's friend, his full flushed face, an improbably small bone held delicately between his fingers. He's going to want me to sleep with him, I thought, and looked down at my plate. Don't laugh now or you'll start to cry. "Why aren't you eating?" he asked.

9. *that dark night*

I woke up with the knowledge that there was a body next to mine in the bed. It wasn't a bad body either, and just when I was starting to get excited I realized that it was only Will, and if I was going to start getting excited over Will, I'd be in real trouble.

"Will?" I said hesitantly.

"Yeah," he said. "What?"

"What the hell are you doing in my bed? Have a sudden change of heart?"

"No, worse. A nightmare."

"Well why didn't you get into bed with Lucy? You always sleep with her when you're having a bad night."

"Tried that. There was already somebody there. Want to hear about my dream or not?"

I reached out and patted my hand over the nightstand until I found the smokes, matches and an ashtray. I set the ashtray on my chest.

"Can I light it?" asked Will and I handed him the smokes and matches. He's like a kid who always wants to push the buttons when it comes to lighting cigarettes.

"Remember that Bette Davis movie where the guy lights two cigarettes and hands her one," he said.

"What's that got to do with anything?" I asked.

"Nothing. I just liked it that's all."

"Tell me about the dream. What happened?"

"Nothing."

"What do you mean nothing?"

"Nothing. I was lying there, and I thought maybe I'd woken up, only everything was so dark, like not even any light coming in from the street."

"That's it?"

"No, that's not it. I heard a voice."

"A voice?"

"Yeah, a voice. And I knew I was dying because I heard Dylan Thomas reciting 'Do not go gentle into that dark night', just like I always knew I would if I was dying."

"Good."

"What?"

"'Do not go gentle into that good night.'"

"Are you sure?"

"Pretty sure."

"Then I guess I wasn't dying."

"Go to sleep, Will."

"Good night."

"Dark night."

10. the big question

Here we all are, caught in that horrific transition period between childhood and middle age. It's a phase, I say, we'll grow out of it. One of these days we'll stop waiting for our real lives to begin and realize that this is it. We may think we're watching the previews, the coming attractions, but this is the movie and it's already half over: the primary characters have been introduced, the tone is set, the interweavings of plot are progressing.

What are we going to be when we grow up? we ask ourselves and each other constantly, incessantly. We all of us fear being the one left behind, the one who doesn't make it, who never becomes but is only one day promising and the next day nothing.

We pretend to want less than we do. In unguarded moments we speak of things like fame and glory, and then quickly cover our naked desires with laughter and self-mocking.

Somebody writes: *What are you going to do with your life?* on the bathroom mirror with a blue eyeliner pencil. It stays there for a week, all of us facing up to our vulnerable morning faces with the big question superimposed. Talk about doubt written all over your face.

11. sympathy pains

Maeve says that sometimes she is scared to even talk to people because they seem so overwhelmingly fragile. When she says this, Nigel makes a gesture like you do in charades when you mean a movie. *Projecting*, he says.

Maeve reminds me of these china figurines my grand-mother used to have — ballerinas made out of bone china with tutus spun out so fine they would crumble between your fingertips.

All of us conspire to protect Maeve, and whenever bad things happen we put off telling her because she will only cry, which just makes things worse. One time Will had a fight with his father over the same old thing, and by the time he got off the phone Maeve was weeping — that spooky crying where she doesn't even make any noise and seems oblivious to the

tears running down her face. Will took her by the shoulders
and shook her, hard, and said: "It's my pain, mine. You can't
have it." Later he was sorry, and he brought her a four-leaf
clover, and she pretended not to see the glue, and then things
were okay again.

12. *a family album*

When I was a kid we used to have an old plush red velvet-
covered album. On the front, affixed with minuscule screws,
was brass lettering which read *Our Family.* The sepia-toned
studio portraits depicted several dozen stiffly-posed matriarchs,
patriarchs, spinster aunts, crazy uncles, and children dressed as
miniature adults stilled into waxworks. All these people, so few
smiling, all unnameable to us now, beyond the reach of living
memory — was this really *Our Family?*

Nigel asleep in the hammock with the cat, also asleep,
curled into a circle of featureless black fur on his belly. Nigel
looks like an angel, or a statue, or a silent movie star when
he's asleep. His face is dappled by the light through the leaves
of the overhanging branch of the tree. One arm dangles over
the edge of the hammock and his fingers are splayed in the
afternoon air, the way one drags a hand through the water to
create a wake behind a slow-moving boat.

Lucy wearing a pair of hideous paisley pyjamas stolen
from Will. Her hair is a rat's nest of slept-on curls and her face

is sleepy soft and pillow creased. In her features is the honeyed befuddlement of a sleepwalking child.

Will in his bartender clothes, sitting in front of his birthday cake, in a birthday boy pose: cheeks puffed out in the moment of making a wish.

Maeve in black lace panties and push-up bra, her hair bound up on wire curlers snaking out around her face. She is sitting on the toilet seat with her foot on the edge of the tub, painting her toenails. A lit cigarette hangs from one side of her mouth and her left eye is squinted shut against the smoke.

A picture of the linoleum in our kitchen, pink and grey squares. This was on the roll of shots from our housewarming party. The picture was taken, it is generally agreed, by Lucy.

Me, wearing a blonde curly wig from Lucy's tickle trunk. I'm also wearing a red sequin dress, helped out by a pair of grapefruit stuffed down the front. I'm ambivalent about this picture — can't decide if I look like a bodacious Mama, like Will says, or a drag queen, like Nigel says.

The clothes drying on the line. There is a progression here from the sensible to the sublime. After the dryer broke it got to be a running game of whose laundry would turn up the most mentionable unmentionables. Will won the prize with a pair of leopard-spotted scanty briefs. He won't say where they came from. Nigel's theory is that Will's mother knitted them.

Will, Lucy, Nigel and Maeve all on the L-shaped couch. A twister game contortion of limbs, heads, torsos. Saturday morning cartoons.

13. *donuts*

We were watching *Paris, Texas* on the late movie and Lucy said: "These guys could be characters in a Sam Shepherd play," and then somebody else said: "Dick-fucking-Tracy." I can't remember who said it, but it doesn't matter. We all said it a lot that summer.

After the movie ended there was nothing else to do but wait for the sunrise. We all went on a quest for the sunrise. Nigel says that quests are strictly a male thing but Maeve and Lucy and I went anyway. We went to the donut shop and had a coffee but the sunrise wasn't there. We were happy in the donut shop. It was a place where we often went together in various combinations and permutations. People knew us there.

I was afraid we were going to miss the sunrise. "When is it?" I'd ask and they'd say: "Soon." It was almost Fall and the dawn was late. The air had begun to smell different than it had all summer. I kept watch out the window, just to make sure it wouldn't slip by us. I hate missing things, like when you look back on a time in your life and realize you were happy but didn't even notice.

We didn't talk that much about what our plans were for the Fall. Will was going to theatre school out west, Lucy was moving in with a boyfriend, Maeve was going to stay with her sister for awhile, and Nigel refused to say what he was going to do. I had rented a bachelor suite downtown. When I was shown the place the landlord kept emphasizing how quiet it was. As though that were an asset. Anyway, we weren't talking about any of that. We were just living in the moment. Waiting for the sunrise. We were acting like the house would always be there for us to go back to.

It wasn't what we expected. Of course, they always say nothing ever is. I wanted a hill to sit on. I wanted maybe a hint of a hangover or the last vestiges of drunkenness. I wanted dew. I wanted to be in love, but that's irrelevant, that's what we wanted all the time. I wanted dew.

SHADOWS AND BORROWED LIGHT

I wake with my head full of borrowed light and wonder is it yesterday or tomorrow. My child's footsteps in the hall, rushing toward my doorway, are what have wakened me. Each morning is alike in this. One of these mornings I will count the number of footsteps from her room to mine. My child is like one only recently bereft of wings. I value her for how little she reminds me of myself, for I see myself as a cracked and crazed pitcher, too often mended.

With two heads to one pillow we fall back into sleep and wake together to the sound of a bee battering itself against the window, trying to find the way out where the way in was so easy.

"Help him," begs my child, my Annalise.

Obediently I rise and throw the window wide. The bee flies out leaving a warm silence behind. Outside, the plum blossoms have blanketed the ground like snow.

Annalise has honey for breakfast. She licks it off her spoon. This can't be good for her. None of this. She needs a more orderly life, a more regular existence. Yet Annalise is four years old and soon will leave me . . . for school, for friends, for a life of her own. For now she is mine, all mine, to indulge as I will.

"What do you think we will do today?" asks Annalise.

"Visit your grandmother," I answer.

"Oh," she says. "Of course."

My child has two shadows. One her own, and one belonging to the child I lost.

I understand that my absent child is dead but sometimes, for days altogether, it seems to me that it is merely elsewhere. Living a normal life. Sometimes, as I am kneading the dough for the bread and feeling it warm and alive beneath my palms, I think if my child were here now I could feed it. I could at least do that much.

My child, my not-first born, seems in the main unaware of her double shadow, although watching her I can't help but wonder if she feels the pull of its weight, on stairs particularly.

My first, of course, was never born.

Annalise tips the honey jar over and cries out in dismay. I turn and we both watch the honey creeping slowly across the table.

I was twenty when Annalise was born, and unhappy. It seemed as though I'd been unhappy for an age. Suddenly, that all fell away from me and I understood why it was that I was here. The transparent mystery of it all. Her need of me was the anchor that held me to this earth.

"Sorry," says Annalise.
"Don't be," I say.

ə

My mother lives on the other side of town in the second-to-top floor of a new development. She is on the fourteenth floor. She can see everything — the city's buildings are her lawn ornaments. Still she is never happy because she says the fact that her ceiling is someone else's floor makes her wake every morning with a clot in her chest like a lump of coal.

When Annalise makes a new picture she is pleased with she takes it to the window and holds it up for granny on the other side of town to see.

My mother tired one day of the twentieth century and took to writing letters and reading novels. My house filled up with the things she would no longer use — the television, the computer, the telephone.

"What about electricity?" I ask. "Heat, water, light?"

"Don't be absurd," she tells me. "But anything which can be communicated in the blink of an eye hardly seems worthwhile."

My mother writes that she is no longer able to place her faith in the elevator, and is, in effect, marooned on the fourteenth floor. The good daughter goes to a local grocery store and sets up an account for delivery orders.

My mother's letters dwell in the past but whose past remains an open question. The letters arrive at my house, weekly at first but daily now. They all have my address but the names are always different. I read them. Read them as a serial novel. I try to think of my mother by her first name. Carol. She signs herself so.

My mother was once in love, or so the letters reveal. I wonder if she thinks this is something I should know. Perhaps she is sending me the letters deliberately. Perhaps she wants to tell me things but doesn't know how.

My mother was in love with a man not my father whom she calls Ray. *Dear Ray*, she writes, *dearest Ray*. She writes of details which I am surprised to find embarrass me. She writes of the smell of his neck, of the length of the days between his visits, of how she loves his broad fingers. My mother was, it seems, once as green and eager as the spring.

I call the store to see if my mother has been ordering food. Today they received a letter requesting milk and angel food cake. That was all.

&

I have a child's rhyme echoing in my head. It begins, "Not last night but the night before . . . " Not last night but the night before I opened the door and there was a woman on the front step weeping. She had my eyes in someone else's head.

"You don't know me," she said. "I'm your mother."

"You're a stranger," I said.

"I understand," she said. "I gave you up." Her eyes were watery, as though she'd been weeping for years.

"You're mistaken," I said. "You've come to the wrong door."

To illustrate my point I closed the door.

I imagined her going home to her house where all the carpets are sodden with tears.

The door is red. I painted it myself last year. I'd originally thought of painting the whole house but then I woke up one day from a dream where I was living inside an old-fashioned refrigerator. Then I painted the front door red and I never had that dream again.

I closed the door on the woman who said she was my mother. It was obvious she was lying.

"Who was it?" asked Annalise.

"A liar," I answered.

The stranger at the door lost her own baby years ago. Somehow her mind has found me and claimed me as her own. My confusion must have drawn her like a scent. This is what I conclude, for although she did not come back again, she haunts me. I see the way her body curls in on itself as though she were an old woman. I imagine that you could pick her up and find her as light as a child.

I know what it is to lose a child. What it is to carry your memories with you like a pocket full of stones. My first child, unborn and unwanted, is like a dream I wake from with only an impression fleeting as a snowflake.

"I would like a sister," says Annalise. "Or else a rabbit."

❧

Annalise and I go to visit my mother. She opens the door and says, "Oh, I wasn't expecting you."

"But Mother," I say, "we always come at this time."

My mother has taken all her white sheets and covered the furniture.

"Ghosts," exclaims Annalise with glee when we enter the apartment.

"Are you going somewhere?" I ask. I am overcome with memories of summer's end when the cabin was closed away for the long cold months ahead.

"No," says my mother. "Not that I know of."

Annalise goes through the rooms touching things and picking up small objects to feel their weight in her small hands. My mother is not bothered by this. She trusts Annalise not to break anything that really matters. Annalise loves all the knick-knacks and bric-a-brac that my mother's apartment contains. The place is like Aladdin's cave to her. And yet, she has many times refused the offer of small china flower baskets, of a votive candle holder that refracts the light, of a box that opens to reveal a smaller box that opens to reveal a yet smaller box. She understands that these objects could so easily lose their magic.

"There is this crazy woman," I tell my mother. "She's been bothering us."

"In what way?" my mother asks and I am ashamed to tell her.

"She has my eyes," I say.

Annalise sits at the piano and runs her fingers lightly over the keys. We have offered her lessons, both my mother and I, but she refuses. "When I am old," she says. Annalise is four years old and the world lies before her like an unfurled bolt of white cloth.

"This woman," says my mother. "It is, most likely, my sister."

"But you have no sister," I say.

Annalise stands at the window straining to see our house beyond the river. Her hair is full of sunlight; it gleams like new pennies.

"No, not now," says my mother.

Sometimes, when Annalise turns her head quickly, as just now, I imagine she will catch sight of the second shadow. The child I killed. I was young and thought I was acting for the best.

"My sister always wanted what I had. She took your father."

"Took him?"

"Took him, had him, what difference does it make now?"

What difference? What difference.

My mother stands to look at herself in the oval mirror above the piano. She has done this several times now since we arrived.

"He didn't stay with her long," says my mother. "If that's any consolation to you. It wasn't to me."

She smooths the fine white hairs away from her forehead and smiles a satisfied smile.

"She was foolish enough to come weeping to my door. Asking if I knew where he'd gone. As if I cared."

My mother is growing into an alabaster perfection. Strange I didn't notice sooner.

My father went away one day when I was quite small. He went off to war, I told the children at school, but they laughed at me. They knew there was no war. I killed him in battle but denied him a good death. He never came back. That much was certain.

Annalise has no father. I wasn't making that mistake twice. She asked me once and I told her that I swallowed a cherry pit and she grew in my belly. I won't say she believed me, but she hasn't asked again.

My father was tall and thin. So thin that I used to imagine folding him up like a blind man's cane.

I wonder who I can believe. There is my father who made himself vanish like a magician disappearing into his own top hat. There is my mother, who day by day grows more unlike the person she once was, and there is this crazy woman who appears at the door carrying her grief and loss like it is something for sale.

I leave my mother lost in the pages of a novel by Edith Wharton. She does not look up as we leave. She will not look up for days. She has abandoned the world and it is both lost and found all at once.

ॐ

In the elevator Annalise strains to reach the buttons. She has yet to forfeit belief in anything.

"I couldn't see our house," says Annalise. "How can Granny see it if I can't?"

"Ah," I say, thinking. "She can only see the house when you are in it. You are the candle in the window."

This satisfies her for the time being. The doors open and we exit.

If the past was a thing I could put into a suitcase then I could carry it with me, or not, as I chose. My daughter has no father and two shadows. Like the sun, she makes her own light. She has what love I can give her. She has plum blossoms, honey and notes in no order. It is enough to go on with.

COMING TO TERMS

It wasn't quite dawn when I got in the car. I was wearing the jeans and shirt I'd thrown off onto a chair the night before and an old cable-knit sweater of Roger's. I hadn't sent the sweater back when the lawyer called for his things. I don't know why. Roger's mother had knitted it for him the first year we were married. When he wore it he looked like the guy in the Irish Spring soap commercial. I was glad that the car had a full tank of gas. I wouldn't have to stop until I hit Prince Albert, and then I'd be almost there. I stopped at all the red lights, even though there were hardly any cars on the road. When I was a little girl I thought my father was magic because he always knew when the light was going to turn. It was years before I caught on to his trick of watching the other light turn red. I cried then, the same way as when I found out about Santa Claus, and when I found out that the summer my mother died he'd been sleeping with her best friend.

It didn't take me long to get out of Saskatoon, and once I left the city behind I stopped thinking about anything. I didn't even turn the radio on. At Duck Lake I stopped and got a coffee. It was lukewarm and tasted of the styrofoam cup. I kept my eyes on the road in front of me. I was running a race and I couldn't allow myself to think of anything until I was home free. At the gas station in Prince Albert I bought a couple of bottles of mineral water and some chocolate bars.

The trees. The trees were always the first sign that we were nearly there. Tall mournful poplars. Once I went to an Ernest Lindner exhibit at the Mendel Art Gallery and it was full of these trees from my childhood. I bought a poster from the show and no matter how many times I looked at I still got the same rising feeling of expectation.

I pulled onto the dirt road for our beach. Our cabin was number forty-two. Only one or two of the cabins before ours had cars in the driveway. Still too early in the year. Most of the cabins weren't winterized and it was still months off from the time when you could actually go in the lake.

The Macphersons' place, the Stillwells', the Cravens'. The old places looked pretty much the same as when I was a kid. It was only the ones that had been sold that had the ugly cedar decks. Then there was our drive, the steep incline that used to scare me silly when I was a kid. Dad would have to stop and let me off on the road before he drove down. I always expected the car to just keep on going and smash right into the back of the cabin. The fact that it never did didn't keep me from believing it was inevitable. I shut off the ignition and then I thought to myself: what are you doing here? But it was too late.

The key was right where it always used to be, under a rock in the old stone barbecue, but when I opened the screen door there was a shiny new padlock on the door. Barbara. It had to be, nobody else would think of it. I walked around to the side of the cabin, where the window of my old bedroom was. At least the window hadn't changed. I got it open okay, but getting myself through it wasn't as easy as it had been when I was a teenager. Inside, the cabin was freezing. The whole winter seemed to be stored up inside.

Both woodboxes had been left filled so I got a fire going in the kitchen stove and then started one in the living room. I had to go back out to the car to get the water — I let myself out the front door that locked from the inside. While I was waiting for the kettle to boil I took a look around. I hadn't been up here for a couple of years. Colin's family spent most of the summers up here — and even though I always had, as Barb said, an open invitation, I had yet to take them up on it. Things looked pretty much the same. I pulled the plastic covers off the living room furniture and dumped them in a corner without folding them. Barb had recovered all the chairs — it was one of her hobbies. They looked horrendous. As though they were trying to be something they weren't.

When the kettle started to whistle I went into the kitchen and made myself a cup of instant. The cupboards were as well-stocked with non-perishables as ever. One point for Barb. I took the coffee outside. Better to leave the fires going for a while and let the cabin warm up. It was warmer out than in and I went down to the beach, cup in hand.

The lake was gray and choppy. The beach looked funny without the dock in. I looked up and down the lake and most people hadn't put theirs in yet either. I got an old wooden deck chair out of the shed and sat down and drank my coffee. The sight of the water breaking on the gravelly beach lulled me, as it always does. I love the water. There was a fine mist over the lake, and it was impossible to see to the far side. It was as if

there were no other side. It could have gone on forever. The
sky and the water were nearly the same dead shade of gray.
In the distance there was the familiar call of the loons.

I stood and picked up a handful of rocks and tried to skip
them across the water. Two. One. Three. Two. I never was
much good at it. The small splashes only made the silence
louder. A gust of wind came along and brought voices from
across the lake. Laughter. I found myself wishing I knew what
the joke was.

By the time I went back up both fires had gone out and
I had to restart them. The cabin was a little warmer, but not
much. I went into the back bedrooms to look for a coat. The
big bedroom, the one that had been Mom and Dad's was Colin
and Barb's now, but when I opened the wardrobe it was still
full of Mom's things. The smell of mothballs and a lighter, fainter
scent — lilac? — escaped and prickled at the inside of my nose.
I pulled out an old Hudson's Bay jacket and quickly shut the
cupboard up again. In the beginning, Dad hadn't had the heart
to throw her things out and eventually they just became part
of the cabin like the jigsaw puzzles with their missing pieces,
the accordion nobody could play, the old copies of *Life* maga-
zine and *Ladies Home Journal.* Cabins don't keep pace with
real life.

I loaded the big water bottles into the back of the car and
drove down to the pump at the end of the beach. I filled all
three bottles but then I couldn't lift them to carry them to the
car so I had to dump half the water out. Even so, I had enough
water to last me a good long time. When I got back I turned
the rain barrel right side up, just in case. I had no idea how
long I was going to stay, but it was best to be prepared. Anyway,

it wasn't as though I had anything to hurry back for. Well, my job, but they were close to letting me go anyway. And it wasn't as though I really wanted to sell flowers. In fact I hated it. Funerals, anniversaries, seductions, apologies. In a long line of bad jobs, it was the worst. All those years putting Roger through school and what did I end up with? Of course, Dad had forced him into giving me a big settlement, but it wasn't the money. It was that there was nothing for me to do.

By evening the cabin had warmed up enough that with the jackets and a blanket I could sit by the fireplace and be pretty certain I wasn't going to freeze to death. In the old ice box that served as a liquor cabinet I'd found five bottles of scotch, Glen Fiddich. What is it with lawyers and scotch? Dad was the same way. I wonder if it's something they teach them at school. There were also an assortment of sticky-sweet liqueurs. Barb's no doubt. Nothing I wanted any part of. Then there were a couple of bottles of wine. I couldn't tell by the label if it was good wine or not. I don't know anything about the stuff. The price tags had been peeled off so I had no way of knowing. I opened one and had it with crackers and beans out of the tin. What goes with beans? Red or white? I went for the white because red always gives me hangovers.

I pulled the settee over by the fire, stacked a pile of magazines from the shelf onto the table and settled in with the wine. When the bottle ran out I switched to scotch. The oldest magazines were at the bottom of the pile. I picked out a bunch from 1960 and I was back to before my mother died. There were ads for the car we drove, a Dodge Dart, there were pictures of women with their hair done up like Mom's had been. They were wearing one-piece bathing suits and smiling. Beautiful, empty smiles.

When I woke up I didn't know where I was. The first thing I saw was the wolfskin stretched out on the opposite wall. It was the deadest thing I'd ever seen. When I was small I'd had nightmares about it until Jamie gave it a name. He called it Duke and he would stand on a chair to stroke the fur on the back of its neck.

I looked around, saw the dead fire, the half-covered furniture. I opened the blinds on the front windows, and the ledges were covered in dead flies. I managed to make it all the way up the path to the outhouse before I got sick. Then I went down to the lake and washed my face in the icy water. When I stood up and turned around there were two RCMP guys standing there.

"Mrs. Macphail?" one asked.

I wiped my face off with the sleeve of my jacket. Mothballs.

"Yes," I said, trying to make my voice firm. "I'm Mrs. Macphail, what can I do for you?"

"Well, sorry to bother you ma'am, but we got a call from your brother in Saskatoon. He asked us to swing by and see if you were here." I noticed how careful he was not to meet my eye. Perhaps he was more embarrassed than I was.

"Well, you've found me," I said. I looked up over their heads at the cabin. If only I'd been inside when they came. I wouldn't have had to answer the door. Oh, but the car. They would've known. The mad trapper. Trapper-ess?

"We understand there's been a family tragedy," said the second man, the one who hadn't spoken yet. What a funny expression, so formal, so old-fashioned.

"That's right," I said. "A death in the family."

"Well, your brother seems very concerned. Would you like us to drive you down to Sunnyside so you can call him?"

Why is there always a cop around when you don't need one. These two were just a couple of kids, so sincere too. I just wanted to be left alone.

"That's fine," I said. "I mean, I'm fine. You don't need to drive me anywhere."

"If you say so, ma'am."

Yes, I say so, and stop calling me ma'am, I thought but I didn't say anything. Just smiled and followed them up the path and watched them get into their car. As they were driving away I waved, a perfectly inane thing to do — but that's what comes from trying to act normal.

That afternoon I drove over to the store and called Colin, collect, from the phone booth. I could have put it on my calling card but I didn't feel like it. The only reason I was calling was I thought he might send the RCs around again and I didn't think I could face it. Colin answered the phone.

"Thank God," he said. "We've all been worried sick."

"Is Jamie there?" I asked.

"Yes, he got in yesterday morning. I told you — "

"No, I mean is he *there*. I want to talk to him."

I heard Colin let out one of his drawn-out sighs as he set down the phone. Some of his mannerisms were so precisely Dad's that I wondered if he hadn't taken them up consciously.

"Margie?"

"Oh, Jamie, thank God. I'm not up to one of Colin's lectures today."

"Don't be too hard on him. It's his way of showing he cares."

"Yeah, I know, like Dad. Is he really dead?"

"Yeah, Margie, he's really dead. Are you okay?"

"I guess so. I mean, I think I am. It just was such a shock. That's a stupid thing to say, isn't it? That's what people always say. I just didn't think the old bastard would actually die. I . . . when's the funeral?"

"Tomorrow. In the afternoon. Do you want me to come and get you?"

"No, no you stay there with Colin. Oh Jamie, it just doesn't make any sense. I keep thinking you're still little boys. You and Colin. Taking the boat out fishing. And sandwiches. Mom would make you sandwiches and put tea in a thermos. Dad out chopping the wood, with his sleeves all rolled up so you could see his muscles. His summer muscles, Mom called them. And at night when we go to bed you hear everybody else going to bed, because the cabin walls are so thin. All of us there together, safe inside. And now . . . I'm just not ready. First Mom and now Dad and we're all alone. They left us all alone."

"Margie, listen to me. You shouldn't be up there by yourself. If I leave now I can be there before dark and we can drive back to the city together tonight."

"No, Jamie. I'll come back tomorrow. I'll show up, even if just so Colin doesn't have to be embarrassed. I promise. Listen, I just have to tell you something."

"What's that?"

"We're still here. On the wall, you remember? Every summer Dad would line us up against the wall and mark off our height for that year. It's still there."

"Margie — "

"No, don't worry. I'm okay. Wait a minute. What about you? Are you okay?"

"Yeah, I am. I just want it to be over. Luckily, Colin's taking charge of everything, you know Colin. You just get home safe okay?"

"Okay. Hey, Jamie, love you like a brother."

"Yeah, you too."

When I got back to the cabin it was freezing cold again. I got the fires going in no time. When I was little and we came up here I was never allowed to make fires. The boys were, though, and it didn't seem to have anything to do with age. My mother was allowed to make kitchen fires, in the stove, but not in the living room fireplace. It was a male domain. Like the boat. Dad taught the boys how to drive the boat, but not me. So then I had to pretend that I didn't want to drive the boat and that I would rather take the canoe out. The truth was that I hated the canoe, it was too slow. The only thing I liked about it was the paddling muscles I developed in my arms. At night I would go to bed and then feel the ache through the backs of my arms and up into my shoulders. They felt the same as growing pains.

I beat Colin at arm wrestling one summer. I was ten and he was eleven. He paid me a dollar not to tell Dad about it. Now I wish I had told because nothing that dollar would've bought me could ever be as satisfying as the look on his face would have been.

Once the kitchen fire was going I broke out the groceries I'd bought at the store over at the beach. The old guy who used to work at the store wasn't there anymore, and his son had taken over the business. The funny thing was that he looked exactly the way Old Man Higgins did when I was a kid. "Mr. Higgins?" I said when he was ringing up my order. He looked up at me and then I realized. Mr. Higgins must have died years ago. "Do I know you?" the son asked. "No," I said. I bought a dozen eggs, bacon, bread, and a bag of apples, and a handful of picture postcards. Pictures of the lake, the beach, elks, bears, loons.

I fried the bacon in one pan and the eggs in another. When the bacon was done I took it out and put the bread in the fat to fry. This was the breakfast that Mom always used to make us up here. I hadn't eaten it since. It wasn't the kind of thing that would ever occur to me in the city. It was an old-fashioned food. A far cry from oat bran and carrot juice. Roger ate porridge every morning of his life. I used to get up just to make it for him. It was one of those things I did for years without ever questioning. Until now. Now everything I ever did seems questionable.

Before I married Roger I thought of going into law. I was doing a bachelor's degree at the U of S and my marks were good, better than Colin's were. Colin was getting ready to write the LSATs and one night I said at dinner: "You know, I've been thinking about law school." Dad said: "Thinking what about it?" And I said that I was thinking of going. He laughed. He laughed so hard there were tears in his eyes. Nothing he could have said would have been worse than his laughter. The next year I married Roger. When I moved out Dad got a housekeeper to do the cleaning and cook his meals. To take my place.

Dad cried the day of my wedding. It was just when we were about to drive to the church. "Your mother would've been so proud," he said, and there were tears in his eyes. Now I wonder what my mother would've been proud of. I was a good girl and I did everything that was expected of me, but is that anything to be proud of? She might have been surprised at the way I turned out though. Up until the time she died I was a terrible tomboy. There was one whole summer where the only name I would answer to was Mike, because I thought Margaret was a sissy name. I refused to read anything but *Boys Own Adventure* books. I threw tantrums when Dad wouldn't let me drive down to the dump with him and the boys to see the bears.

If my dead mother should be proud of anything it should be of that one summer when I showed some of what my father liked to call the Turner grit. She was good to me that summer. Nights, after all the lights were out I could hear her telling my father that I'd grow out of it. Not to worry. She let me wear Colin's old dungarees and sneakers, and made the boys do all the same chores that I did. If I had to wash dishes, they had to do dishes and if they had to do yardwork, then I did too. It ended one day when Dad came in as Jamie and I were doing up the breakfast dishes, both wearing old aprons of Mom's. Flowered ones. He hit the roof.

After I finished eating I went out to the kitchen to do up my dishes. Then I thought of Dad and the yardwork I was never allowed to do again, and how everything came down to boys and girls, and the difference which should be obvious, but never was to me. Instead of doing the dishes I threw my plate and fork into the garbage can. It would drive Barb crazy. There wouldn't be even numbers of anything, and the sets were too old to buy replacements. She'd probably have to throw them all out and buy new. She was like that. It was one of the things I couldn't stand about her.

I could never figure out how somebody could be happy married to my brother Colin, but Barb seemed to be. She always phoned me the week before their anniversary to remind me because, as she said, Colin would be so hurt if I forgot. When Roger and I got divorced I'm sure she went to the card store to see if there was anything appropriate for the occasion. For my birthday that year she bought me flannel pyjamas that looked as though they were made for a twelve year old. As if she thought I'd been de-sexed. For her birthday the next month I went out and bought her these horrid sleazy baby dolls. I couldn't stop laughing thinking how much Colin would hate them.

Thinking about Colin and Barb, about my father and mother, about Roger suddenly made me feel terribly tired. Families weren't supposed to be this way. I wasn't sure how they were supposed to be, but I knew this wasn't it. I went to get a drink from the icebox and my eye was caught by the markings on the wall beside it. They started when I was five, Jamie was four and Colin was six, the summer the family bought the cabin. Mom died in 1962. Up until then we marked off every year, but after that they became sporadic. Randy and Shelley's names were there, Colin's kids. The dates for Mom and Dad were from the year they bought the cabin. I stood up against the wall and put my hand to the top of my head. When I turned

I saw that I was exactly the same height my mother had been. I was standing there looking at the wall when I heard the kitchen door open.

My first thought was that Colin had sent the RCs to get me, but then Jamie called out. "Mike? You here?"

I walked into the kitchen and Jamie was standing there holding the padlock in his hand.

"Barb gave me the key," he said.

"Why'd you call me Mike?" I asked. "You haven't done that in years."

"Seemed the thing to do," he said. "Aren't you going to say you're glad to see me?"

"Haven't decided yet," I said. "But come on in. I'll fix you a drink and think about it."

Jamie wanted to drive back to the city that night but I convinced him it would be better to wait and leave early in the morning. "It will rain," he said. It always rains the last day.

We sat at the dining room table and played Crazy Eights and drank Colin's scotch. Jamie didn't like scotch much either but we both drank it. I asked him about the wine and he said that it wasn't very good stuff which made me feel better somehow. Jamie said that he and Colin had a fight about whether or not it should be an open coffin at the funeral, but he didn't say anything else about it except that the service was at two o'clock.

"Colin told me to make sure you wear a dress," he said with a small smile.

"Doesn't he think I know how to behave at all?"

"I guess not."

I drew a card and looked at the cards in my hand. For a minute I couldn't remember what game we were playing.

"Remember Mom's funeral?" I asked.

"Of course," he said.

"Colin didn't cry. I couldn't understand that. I've never been able to understand that."

"You shouldn't be so hard on him," Jamie said. "He's had a tough time living up to the old man."

"Didn't we all?"

"I don't know. I gave up a long time ago."

Jamie runs an interior design shop in Vancouver. The only thing our father ever said about it was that he thought that only those "light in their loafers fellows" went in for that kind of thing.

"He was a real bastard," I said. I discarded from my hand without looking at the cards.

"You're thinking about Louise, aren't you?" he said.

"No," I said. "I wasn't." I hadn't been really, but she was always there just the same. When I remembered the summer my mother died I remembered Louise. She and her husband owned a cottage down the beach from ours and in Saskatoon they had lived three houses down. She had a daughter a year older than me and a son a year younger. The daughter was a foxy-faced girl with fingernails chewed down to the nubs. She told me that my mother was going to die, that she'd heard them talking, that there was nothing that could be done to save her. I thought she was lying. When I found out it was true I never spoke to her again. Louise was my mother's best friend.

"I think there may be something about Dad and Louise that you don't know," Jamie said. "I was talking to Colin about it today and he finally told me."

"What? That it didn't happen? That we didn't see what we saw?"

"No, it happened all right. But after. After Mom died. Not before. We thought it had been going on a long time, but it hadn't. It never happened again. Just that once."

"Is that supposed to make it all right?" I put my cards down face up on the table. I couldn't keep anything straight.

"Maybe it doesn't make it any easier to forgive him, but I think it makes it easier to understand. Mom was dying for a long time, longer than we knew. It must have been hell for him to watch that, not to be able to do anything to stop it."

I gathered up all the cards and put them back in the box.

"I'm going down to the lake," I said. "You can come if you want."

I was halfway down the path when I heard the screen door fall shut. I turned and saw Jamie standing there. He was wearing one of the old Siwash jackets and he looked like a boy. We walked down to the shed where the old wooden boat was and, silently, he helped me drag it down to the beach. I flipped it over and Jamie watched to see what I was going to do. The rocks on the beach scraped against the bottom of the boat. I got in and sat at the back, beside where the motor was supposed to go. The driver's seat. Jamie got in and sat at the front, at the bow, and laid himself down on one of the bench seats, hanging his feet over the side.

"Maybe I don't want to understand him," I said. Jamie put his arms up behind his head and looked at the sky. I couldn't find the words to tell him that I had no room to grieve for anyone else and it was easier not to forgive.

When we were children our boat was the fastest on the lake. Now it was just an old wooden shell, the lacquer half chipped away, the oar-wells all smashed up, the oars themselves long lost.

I looked up at the sky, wishing there were some way to unravel time and memory, to make everything come out the way you wanted. The northern lights were out and I looked at Jamie to see if he saw them too. He nodded and didn't say anything, and for a while we both just watched the skies, the colours dancing.

"Makes you believe," I said, finally, in a half-whisper.

"Believe in what?" asked Jamie, and he was whispering too.

"I don't know," I said. "But it does. It makes you believe."

JENNY'S IUD

Jenny is going to be famous one day, you can tell just by looking at her. It's hard to say what she might get famous for because just being Jenny should be enough. I'm keeping notes and one day I'll write the story of her life. The best parts are the ones she makes up.

Jenny is getting her life together bit by bit. She says it's like doing a jigsaw puzzle only without the picture on the box to go by.

Jenny has forgotten how to sleep. It used to be so easy, she says. I never even had to think about it. Since she's started thinking about it she can't do it anymore. It's like swimming she says. When she thinks about the water holding her up she always sinks. She won't fly because she believes the main cause of crashes is people who don't believe the air will hold the plane up.

Jenny lets men in bars buy her drinks. When I tell her that they are going to expect something she just laughs and says that's their problem. Jenny and I always dance the last dance together and walk out of the bar arm in arm.

Jenny used to have a family like everybody else but she claims to have misplaced them. She says when she was twelve the family was moving cross country with a truck and a U-Haul, and they forgot her at a gas station on a bathroom break. Jenny doesn't hold a grudge about this; she says when they realized she wasn't in the back they probably turned around and came back for her. The thing is, by that time she'd already got into somebody else's car.

Jenny can sing like Bessie Smith when she's drunk. I tell her she should be a singer and go on the road but she says it would turn her into an alcoholic. She can't sing when she's sober; she opens her mouth and nothing comes out.

Jenny used to read Tarot cards but she saw a death in the cards that came true and so she stopped. She always knows what's going to happen next; sometimes she tells me and other times she doesn't. She's my guardian angel and she lets me know on days when it's not safe to go out of the house. On these days we stay in bed and eat jam sandwiches and make up stories for each other.

Jenny has a fear of electrical appliances. She won't use the stove, or curl her hair with a curling iron, or vacuum even when it's her turn. She thinks that she was electrocuted in a previous life. She even thinks she might have got the chair for something.

Jenny doesn't do anything for a living and I don't know where her money comes from. Every month's end when I ask her if she's going to be able to make rent she answers: "the universe will provide." I'm not sure what this means. It could mean that she rides the subway at rush hour and picks peoples' pockets. I don't ask.

Jenny used to work as an artist's model and pose in the nude. I think she is the most beautiful woman I have ever known. She likes being naked and walks around the house that way. I think it's a gift that Jenny has; she can be naked better than anybody I know. She has scars all over her torso but she won't say where she got them. I have nightmares about them.

Jenny gets thrown out of museums and galleries for caressing the sculptures. You have to feel them, she says. You have to pretend you're blind. Once she got caught licking a painting to see how it tasted.

Jenny is never bored; she says she tried it one time and she didn't like it. She is always thinking about something and if you ask her she'll tell you what it is. I try not to ask too often because that would spoil it, so I wait until she's being real quiet and has a funny look on her face. Then she'll tell me things like Bette Davis's grandson stuck a peanut up his nose and lost thirty percent of his hearing. One time she told me that she'd connected all the moles on her stomach and they made a fish.

Jenny makes lists all the time and leaves them all over the house for anyone to see. Sometimes they don't say anything interesting, just junk: water the fern, buy tampons, get a haircut. Other times they are lists of people she's slept with, or means to write letters to, or thinks she was in past lives. Once I found a piece of paper that said THINGS TO DO and underneath: Tell Janna that I love her. She never did but the next day the list was still there with its single entry crossed out so I guess she figured I already knew.

Jenny is the kind of person things happen to. Strange things. She says that she used to walk around with a victim sign on her back, but doesn't anymore. She's seen more flashers than anyone I know. She sees ghosts too, and recently she told me that her IUD was picking up signals from outer space again.

Jenny thought she was losing her mind one time. She was in a public washroom and staring at all the faces in the mirror above the sinks and couldn't figure out which one was hers. Maybe this never happened to her, she says. Maybe she only saw it in a movie, but it's still a bad sign.

Jenny talks about getting out, moving somewhere new and starting over. I go real quiet when she talks this way because I don't want her to ever leave. Sometimes, even with other people in the room, I feel like I'm alone, but never with Jenny. She's one of those people who can hear you even when you're not talking.

EDITH AND THE SECONDHAND DREAM

S ofie is thinking of the night it must have happened. When
Edith didn't come home after school she'd been worried,
but also pleased. Edith deserved a life of her own — friends,
a boyfriend, all of those things. But the next morning when
Edith wouldn't meet her eye and then lied and said she'd been
at Darlene's, Sofie was unable to say: I heard you in the store
last night. Who is he? She couldn't say or ask any of the things
she wanted to.

The bell rings above the door when Edith comes in. The
store is empty of customers and strangely quiet. The place is
full of history, but it all belongs to strangers.

"Edith, I'm so glad you're home." Sofie comes out of the
back room, wiping her hands on her dress. "There was a man
just in here. He looked just like your father. Exactly like. Dark
wavy hair and a smile that would melt an iceberg."

Why start that business again, Edith thinks. *You look like
your father,* Sofie tells her, but Edith has no way to know for
sure if it is or isn't true. Edith wonders what her mother looked

like when she was young. Sofie is small and round and pale. Her hair is light blonde, too light to distinguish any beginnings of grey. She wraps it tightly on curlers each night and all day long the curls sit there in her head as tightly as if the curlers were still in them.

Edith sees nothing of herself in her mother. Beside her she feels too tall, as though her hands and feet are grotesquely large. Her colouring is dark, unlike her pale English rose of a mother. She think she looks like someone else's child.

There are no pictures of her mother and father together, or of Edith as a child. There are no pictures at all of her father. Sofie says they were lost. The pictures on their walls upstairs come from the shop. Pictures of other people's children. If Edith could just see a picture of herself with her mother and father, she tells herself, everything would make sense.

"I'm going to bed, Ma, I'm not feeling so well."

Edith knows she'll be unable to sleep, but cannot sit silent with her mother and does not trust herself to speak. She lies in bed with the light off, listening for the sound of her mother coming up the stairs. She does not sleep until she hears a hiss of static from the television and her mother's gentle snore.

Sofie sits in the chair by the cash register. She's had the chair so long that the arms curl around her. Between the arms and the cushion are stashed half-empty packs of cigarettes, bags of humbugs gathering lint, and romances taken from the shelves to read.

Against the wall are racks of men's and women's clothes with boxes stacked on the floor beneath them. She washes all the clothes herself in the old washer upstairs. But some of them are dry clean only, the men's suits and the ladies' fancy dresses. No amount of lemon deodorizer will cover the heavy air of perspiration, stale cologne and mothballs that drifts up the stairs to the small rooms she and Edith share.

She has a sweater tucked under the counter to give to Edith. It is cashmere and hand-beaded with tiny pieces of black jet. Sofie knows it is not something Edith would wear but can't help thinking how beautiful she would look.

In the locker room Edith dresses with her back to the other girls. She refuses to shower. Her classmates bounce around in their underwear trying to find enough electrical outlets for their curling irons and fighting for space at the mirrors. Behind the open door of her locker Edith steps into her slacks and blouse; the blouse pulls and gapes at the button between her breasts. Over the blouse she pulls on an old navy cardigan of her mother's which hangs loosely about her hips.

She doesn't turn when she hears Gordie's name. Shelley is saying that he has asked her to go steady. The other girls giggle and say, " . . . and we all know what that means." *They don't know the half of it,* thinks Edith. She picks up her books and slams out the door, leaving the laughter behind her.

She is early for her English class. She will get the other girls in trouble. Mr. Sharpe will say: *Why is it that Edith can be on time and the rest of you can't?* She sits on the floor in the hallway, sucking on the end of her braid and watching the slow hands of the clock on the opposite wall. She waits for the other girls to come rushing down the hall and pass by her.

In her desk at the back of the room she opens her notebook and marks off another day on the inside front cover. She turns to a blank page and tries to listen to Mr. Sharpe. He is telling them to open their poetry anthologies to page 67. Edith has forgotten her book at home again. She raises her notebook so that he will not notice and tell her to share a book with one of the other girls. She counts the lines of blue ink on the page.

Edith has promised to mind the store after school. Sofie has another appointment with the doctor about the dry rattle in her chest that keeps her from sleeping nights.

"Do you know where I left my keys this time?" Sofie asks as Edith comes through the door. She is pulling things from her purse and dumping them into a pile on the counter. Edith rings up NO SALE on the cash register and takes the keys from the drawer as it opens.

"Thanks. I don't know what I'd do without you. There are boxes in the back to be unpacked if you have time. Bye."

Edith enjoys unpacking boxes. Her mother will often buy stuff sight unseen. Someone will call up and say: my mother died . . . I'm moving . . . I was just cleaning some junk out of the basement . . . and Sofie will buy it for ten bucks a box. She says she makes her money from people who are unable to face their past. There's no such thing as junk, Edith, she will say. Everything is worth something to somebody.

The bell rings and Edith reluctantly leaves the half-opened box. It's Gordie. Hands in pockets. Shoulders drawn up.

"What do you want, Gordie?"

"Hey, c'mon now. Is that any way to be?"

"I heard about you and Shelley," she says. "So there's not much point in you coming around here anymore."

"Edie," he says, and moves toward her.

She's always wanted to be called Edie. Edie was someone magically different. She would have her name stitched on her school jacket with satin thread. She would sneak smokes in the can with the other girls. Edie would wear her boyfriend's promise ring.

She backs away from his touch, positions herself behind the counter. Gordie stops in the middle of reaching for her, shrugs and turns away with a tight smile. The bell rings as he leaves.

When Sofie gets back she is surprised to find Edith still in the shop. She is sitting in Sofie's chair with a box open at her feet.

"Hi, Ma." Edith looks up, guiltily. "I guess I was daydreaming. The doctor have anything new to say?"

"Another prescription, that's what he had to say. Just money in the druggist's pocket. Probably just damn sugar pills."

"Placebos."

"Yeah, them. He says it's all in my head. 'Feels more like my chest,' I says to him. Damned young smart-ass. Thinks he knows everything."

Sofie paces the room, touching the books on the shelves. When she holds a book in her hand she can see the person who used to own it. Edith has inherited this habit of telling lives by touching objects that belonged to people. With books it is mostly a sense of an emotional reaction. Clothes, before they are washed, can sometimes relay a picture of places. Mirrors will sometimes contain a second ghostly reflection. Edith was ten years old before she realized this second sense was unusual, that not every one had it.

"Edith, can you close up again? I just want to drag my poor old body off to bed. That's my good girl." She allows her hand to rest on Edith's hair for a second.

Sofie makes her way slowly up the stairs. She should go back down and tell Edith not to worry, she'll close. But she's so weary. The bus ride downtown, the press of people every-where. If she's still awake when Edith comes upstairs she will sit her down and talk to her. What's going on? she'll ask. She will let Edith tell her what she already knows.

Edith trips over something in the dark, looking for the lamp. Sofie is always moving the furniture around, and hauling stuff upstairs if it's been sitting in the shop too long. She finds the lamp and switches it on. The bulb fizzles and pops and then it is dark again.

She turns on the television, setting the volume so that she can just hear it. She pads into the kitchen and takes out the bread. No dirty dishes in the sink. Sofie hasn't eaten. She creeps down the hall and stands outside her mother's door until she can make out the sound of her breathing.

The toast has popped up when she returns to the kitchen. She spreads strawberry jam on it, picking out the lumps of strawberries and putting them back in the jar.

She drags the LAY-Z-BOY up close to the TV so that she can hear it without turning up the volume and takes the afghan from the back of the couch to spread over her legs. She flips the channels past the sit-coms and cop shows until she finds an old movie. She watches for a minute, chewing her toast, and then realizes that she can't understand what they're saying because they're speaking French. The camera moves in on the heroine's face, bathed in light, and as the hero moves in to kiss her the picture closes to a circle and the word *Fin* scrolls across the screen.

She's been holding back thoughts of Gordie all night. He'd never given her a chance to talk to him, but maybe that was just as well because she didn't know what she would have said.

"I'm pregnant," she says to the empty room. Then is embarrassed by the sound of the words when she says them aloud. When she hears them said.

I forgot to give her the sweater, thinks Sofie. She can hear the music from the closing credits of the movie Edith has been watching. She lies very still and she can hear everything. But she cannot go to her.

Edith wakes to the sound of her mother dressing in the next room. She hears the rustle of the dress as her mother puts it on and can almost see her, because all her dresses look alike. Housedresses she calls them. Shapeless, floral printed bags.

She spans her fingers across her belly and presses them into the soft flesh. Should she tell her mother that she thinks she's pregnant? But Sofie would ask how it happened and Edith isn't sure. Not that she doesn't know how it happened, just that she isn't sure why she let it happen. Why she didn't stop him.

"Get in," he'd said, "I'll drive you." She told him where she lived but he didn't drive her straight home. Instead they just drove around and finally ended up at a pizza place on the other side of town. She wanted to phone her mother but thought she'd look like too much of a kid.

Neither of them talked much all night. When he finally drove her home, he stopped the car in front of the store and took the keys from the ignition. "Aren't you going to ask me in?" he asked.

They'd made love on the old horsehair sofa at the back of the store where the lights from the street didn't reach. Made love. She'd given in to him, but it wasn't what she wanted. All she really wanted was for him to go on holding her and whispering *Edie* in her ear. When he got more demanding she didn't know how to stop him. She was afraid to cry out because her mother would hear and come downstairs.

"Edith?" Her mother's voice reaches her through the thin wall. "Time to get up, you'll be late for school if you don't get a move on."

"I'm up," Edith shouts back, and then drags herself from her bed.

Sofie listens for the sounds of Edith getting ready. She hears the bureau drawers open and slam. She hears Edith's bare feet on the linoleum in the hall. She hears the bathroom door shut, and Edith's slow sigh.

Tell me.

As she walks down the main hall Edith wishes she could do something to keep her breasts from bouncing, to keep the eyes from following her. She clutches her books to her chest and walks with her head down.

She's early for biology and the lab is still empty. She opens her notebook to the front cover and marks off another day. The days are marked in little bundles of sticks. Five days to the school week, and every bundle of five is worth seven because she doesn't count on weekends. She doesn't dare count at home. There are three bundles. She is over three weeks late. Is it too early for a doctor to tell? She doesn't want to see a doctor, doesn't need to. She knows.

Sofie opens the shop at nine a.m., the same time that Edith's first class starts. A copy of Edith's schedule is taped to the counter below the cash register. First period today — biology. Sofie turns to the calendar from *Sammy's Kitchen* hanging on the wall. She saves calendars and each year checks her perennial chart and finds an appropriate year. She counts off the days. Her thumb leaves a grimy impression on each of the squares.

Edith catches Gordie staring at her, and when he sees her looking he turns away and whispers something to Chuck. Edith looks back down at her open book and the diagram of the root systems of plants.

The bell rings and she gathers up her books. Gordie stops at her desk. "Hey, listen, Edie, I'm sorry about the other day," he says so quietly she has to strain to hear. "I have to talk to you about — "

The guys have caught up to him; they push him so that he loses his balance and his hands land on Edith's shoulders and she feels his weight press down on her for a second. The guys all laugh and Mr. Parkinson looks up to see what's going on. Gordie shrugs and walks away.

She wishes his hands on her hadn't reminded her of the other time. How nice he was at first and then how cold and abrupt. "C'mon, Edie, you can't get pregnant the first time." But she knew from the very first minute. And from then on only the waiting mattered.

Sofie is waiting for Edith to come home, and she is thinking of her own mother. How her love was a book of rules. When Sofie got pregnant she ran away from home. Ran to the city where she knew no one and no one knew her. It wouldn't be like that for Edith. Edith had her, could count on her understanding. Surely she knew that. Surely it didn't have to be said.

When Edith does come home all Sofie can think to say is, "You look so much like your father, Edith. He was such a handsome man."

"I'm going upstairs to make us supper, Ma. Phone if you need me."

"It's not that busy. I'll just sit here and think my thoughts." She doesn't look up when Edith leaves. As close as she can figure it only happened the once, but sometimes once is all it takes.

I could keep the baby, Edith thinks as she scrambles the eggs in the pan. He would be all mine. The phone rings and she jumps, burning her hand on the skillet.

"Edith? It's Gordie."

"Gordie?"

"Listen, I was wondering if I could come by later. We could take in a show or something. Edie? You there?"

"Yeah. Yeah, I'm here. I don't know Gordie. What about Shelley?"

"Don't worry about her. Meet me down in the shop at half past eight, okay? Gotta go. Bye, Edie."

Sofie notices that Edith has washed her hair while she was waiting for Sofie to come up for supper. She thinks of giving her that sweater now, but guesses it wouldn't be right. They sit across the table from each other, both staring at their food and pushing it around on their plate.

Sofie says, "Tell — " but breaks off.

Edith looks at her. "You look tired, Ma. I think you're working too hard."

"Maybe you're right. I think I'll go to bed early tonight," she says. *Tell me.*

Gordie's car is parked on the street outside the front door when Edith sneaks down to the shop. She unlocks the door without turning on any of the lights. Gordie gets out of the car; she sees him in the circle of light from the streetlamp.

"Where you been, Edie? I thought you maybe changed your mind or something," he says as he walks past her into the shop.

"Should we go?" Edith is buttoning her jacket and starting out the door.

"No, it's too late. We missed the show. Why'n't we just sit down a minute. Talk or something."

Edith re-locks the door. Gordie sprawls on the horsehair sofa, arms outstretched across its back. She takes off her jacket and sits beside him. One outstretched arm falls across her shoulder.

"I don't think this is a good idea, Gordie. Maybe you better just leave. What about Shelley? I thought you two were going steady?" Edith notices the smell of horsehair. Was that there all along?

"That bitch. She don't know nothing. Not like you, Edie. You're something special, Edie, you're different from the other girls. You're, I don't know, more mature. Yeah, real mature." He cups his hand under her breast and laughs low in his throat.

"I thought you wanted to talk, Gordie." She wishes they were somewhere else. She's always felt safe in the store; now she just feels exposed.

"We can talk later." He is unbraiding her hair.

"Now. I want to talk now. Are you going steady with Shelley or aren't you?"

"Going steady — that's a killer. D'ya know what that means? Means she wears your football jacket, expects you to call her every night, means she wants one of those mini-dot diamond rings to prove your love." His lip curls. "It also means she ain't putting out until she's got you where she wants you. I don't need all that crap and I told her so too."

Edith tries to pull away but his hands are tangled in her hair. "Listen Edie," he says, "you don't have to worry. I brought something this time." She pushes his hands away from her.

Sofie can't sit still. She paces the shop, her hands glancing over objects. Telling lives. All she gets today is fragments. Edith wouldn't eat breakfast today. She stayed in her room until it was time to leave for school. Sofie sits on the couch. Edith. The chintz scratching at the backs of her bare legs.

Slut.

Edith is changing her clothes after gym when the word is thrown at her back.

"Well, I guess we all know what sport Edith is best at," says Shelley. "I guess she's just too tired from all the exercise she's getting nights to keep up with the rest of us in gym. Right, Edith?" The other girls are quiet, watching Edith and waiting for her to react.

Edith slams her locker door and runs from the room. She is still wearing her sweatsuit. Her clothes, jacket and purses are all back in her locker. She figures she can wait in the downstairs bathroom until the girls have gone to their next class and then sneak back for her stuff and leave. She wants to go home and crawl into bed. She wants her mother to sit beside her and stroke her hair back from her forehead and say: it will be okay, baby. Like when she was a child.

On her way down the stairs she runs into Mr. Sharpe.

"Something wrong, Edith?" he asks. "Shouldn't you be getting ready for your next class? You are coming to class aren't you? Otherwise I'll have to report you." Mr. Sharpe is a new teacher and not much older than the grade twelve students.

"Go ahead, report me. And while you're at it, tell them I quit. I hate this damn place."

Edith runs out the nearest set of doors. They open into the parking lot, where a group of boys are leaning against the back fence, smoking. Gordie is among them. He meets her eyes and turns away.

Sofie is with a customer when Edith comes home. She gives Edith a questioning look but doesn't say anything as she runs through the store and up the back stairs.

Edith locks the bathroom door behind her and turns on the faucets in the tub. She lets the water run until it has turned from rust coloured to clear and then puts the plug in the drain. She pulls off her runners and socks and then takes off the sweatsuit, balls it up and throws it against the door.

She stands in front of the mirror in her bra and panties. She can feel an ache at the base off her back and a dull pain pressing in on her belly. She unhooks her bra, lets it fall to the floor and cups her hands beneath her breasts. They feel full, heavy. She turns away from the mirror, bends to pull her panties off and sees the spots of blood.

She eases herself into the hot water. The tub is cold against her back. Her feet and legs are turning pink from the heat.

"Edith?" Sofie is banging on the door. "Edith, let me in. Are you okay? Edith?"

She lies with her ears beneath the water so that all she can hear is her own heart beating.

THE UNEXAMINED LIFE

Jane stopped sleeping. For nights and nights instead of sleeping she would lie rigid on her side of the bed with her eyes closed. When Cal started to softly snore she'd open her eyes and by the light of the streetlamp outside their front window peer at the map on the ceiling.

It resembled the map of the London Underground as she remembered it from the trip they took when they were first married. Not a honeymoon, they never used that word. This map was like that one in that it featured lots of snaking and tangled lines of different colours, but it was different in that it was a map of not a place but a life. It was the map of Jane's life.

"Are you okay?" asked Cal.

"What do you mean?"

"Just what I said. Are you okay?"

"Why wouldn't I be? Don't I seem okay?"

"Maybe you should see a doctor."

"I have. She says it's nothing."

Every morning after Cal left for his job at the school, Jane had fifteen minutes to search the house before she had to leave for her job at the bookstore. He was a principal. He and Jane had been in education together but in the end she found she couldn't cut it in the classroom. That was how Cal had put it to her. "You can't cut it," he said. "Admit it now and move on." So she gave up her position and went to work in the bookstore and was much happier. More relaxed.

Jane wondered how long Cal had been having the affair. That mattered more than who with. Or it mattered at least as much. She hadn't found any evidence yet but eventually he would slip up. *They always do,* she thought. Like the murderers in detective stories. There's always that one oversight.

She carefully raised each piece of his clothing to her face and inhaled before dropping it into the washing machine. She went over phone bills and credit card bills item by item. She read his daytimer as though it was a novel in a foreign language. And still she learned nothing. But it was obvious that he must be seeing someone else.

The bookstore was small and hardly anyone ever came in. Even the boss was never there. Jane often suspected it must be a front for something, but what? When she arrived that morning the phone was ringing.

"It's me," said Cal.

"I thought you were at work."

"Of course I'm at work. Where else would I be. I called to say I won't be home for dinner. Meetings."

"Right."

"I'll make it up to you. Tomorrow we'll go out. You choose the place."

"Remember the time we lost each other in London. On the subway?"

"I don't have time, now. We'll talk later."

"What was I wearing?" Jane asked him.

"When?"

"The first time we met."

"You . . . I don't know. It was so long ago. But wait, I remember, you had your hair all tied back. It was long then and it made a beautiful river down the centre of your back."

"Really? You really remember that?"

"Of course."

There were days in the bookstore when she did not use her voice for hours on top of hours. When the phone did ring she said, Hello, hello, hello, before she picked up the receiver and said, "Hello, Northern Lights Books." Once Cal surprised her by coming into the bookstore when she thought he was at work. When the bell rang and she looked up she saw a customer. He had a tonsure like a monk and wore a coat buttoned to the chin although there was only a slight chill in the air. Poetry, Jane said to herself, confessional poetry. And then of course she realized it was Cal. Her husband. The man she saw every day. And she wondered when he had grown so hungry looking.

A man came into the bookstore and began to ask for novels.

"The store is organized alphabetically," said Jane and pointed out the shelves marked fiction.

"*Madam Bovary*," said the man. He was neatly dressed in a dark suit but the cuffs of his shirt were fraying. Jane didn't know that shirt cuffs really did that . . . it was like suits worn shiny in old novels, suits made of some material she couldn't identify.

"Pardon," said Jane.

"I've always meant to read *Madam Bovary* or do I mean *Anna Karenina*," said the man. "Perhaps now is the time."

"Perhaps," said Jane, but the man read the doubt in her voice.

"What do you think," he asked, and then started again to place more emphasis this time on the word *you*, "what do you think I should read?"

He was like someone who had come to the doctor seeking relief for an unspecified ailment. Jane was tempted to laugh but did not. Instead she walked over to the fiction section and pulled down one of her favourite novels.

"Start with that," she said. "See what you think."

"*Wuthering Heights*," said the man. He practically whispered the words as though he were in church. "I've heard of this," he said.

It was only after he left that she realized she'd forgotten to charge him and she put some money from her own pocket into the till. It was her only sale that morning.

Jane remembered how in their very early days of sharing a bed, she had woken one morning to find that she and Cal had been sleeping with their hands clasped, their fingers all entwined. It gave her a thrill to think that unconsciously one of them had reached out in the night to find the other. Holding hands in public was not one of the things they did. They weren't children after all. They didn't need that show of public affection to define themselves as a couple. It only happened that once but she never forgot it.

When Jane went to the doctor about her insomnia she hoped for a sleeping draught. She knew it is only prescribed in old novels but there was something so tempting in the sound of it. The doctor asked if anything was bothering her and Jane had to think for a long time before answering. The doctor, a woman, was younger than Jane. Jane considered whether she should've tried medical school. Or perhaps a more straightforward field like optometry. The doctor repeated the question and, startled, Jane replied, "No, nothing."

The doctor told Jane that it was possible that she was only dreaming that she wasn't sleeping. "But I'm so tired all the time," said Jane. "Because you think you should be," said the doctor. "But doesn't it amount to the same thing?" asked Jane.

It was Cal who decided that the classroom wasn't the place for her but it was Jane who chose the bookstore. Most days were quiet and she had lots of time to think. When she started the job she used to hear a faint hum or buzz, like the noise a refrigerator makes in the middle of the night when you can't sleep, but after being at the store for a few years she didn't notice it any more. Briefly, during her first year working there, she had an idea that it was the books that were giving out the sound. Resonating.

Sometimes she finds herself doodling on the back of the receipt book, a pattern resembling the map she'd imagined of her life. She thinks about all the lines she never followed, turns she never took, stations she never arrived at.

She thinks if she had a daughter she might name her Emily or perhaps Colette, and if she had a son she would choose Jude.

She thinks that if Cal is unfaithful she will leave.

She thinks that if the man who took *Wuthering Heights* ever comes back it will be a sign.

She thinks that she and Cal will soon be old enough to be parents to the pair who held hands in that long-ago bed.

ALL I EVER WANTED WAS THE MOON

1.

I asked him if he would stay the night. It's nice sometimes to wake up with your arm all pins and needles from being beneath someone's head all night long.

"I can't," he said.

"Just sleep, I mean. That's all."

"I know," he said. "I still can't."

Tom and I had a relationship based on give and take; I gave and he took. We had all sorts of unspoken agreements, including that I wouldn't phone him at home and he wouldn't show me pictures of his kids.

"Tea?" I asked. He nodded and I went into the kitchen to put the kettle on. When I came back he was pacing in circles around my small living room and staring at the pictures on the walls as if he'd never seen them before. His hand went up to stroke the beard he'd shaved off months before.

"Jacquie and I — " he said.

I'd always wondered what she looked like, and if maybe she looked a little bit like me, or I like her. I'd found short red hairs on Tom's clothes a few times and when I asked him if he owned an Irish Setter he'd said no. I wondered other things about her too. If I might have liked her if we had met by chance, at the foreign film night at the library for instance, and shared a coffee afterwards. If we might have found a common bond like that we both had divorced parents, or thought that wearing black made us look thin, or that we both liked the same type of man. And maybe after we'd been through however many Fellini or Truffaut films together, and shared however many coffees or even cappuccinos, maybe after all that shared experience she would have said: *you really must come by for supper one evening and meet my husband and the kids.* And maybe I would have gone.

It's hard not to be angry with Tom for denying me this as well. A friendship between women is one of those things that can carry you through adolescence and menopause and other bad days.

"Sorry, I wasn't listening," I said, and walked past Tom into the kitchen. I started getting the tea things out and clattering cups into saucers.

"Ruth," he said. He touched me softly from behind, his hand tentatively circling the space between my shoulder blades — the buds of my wings my mother called them when I was young.

"I said that Jacquie and I are going away for a while and we're going to try and make things work."

I wondered if he called her Jacquie when they made love or simply "luv" as he did me.

"I told her about us," he said. "I promised her it's over."

"I know," I said. And the kettle began to whistle so I made the tea.

2.

I was having coffee in the Starlight Cafe down the street from my place one night about a week after Tom left. It was the first time I'd been out of the house since I'd dyed my hair red. I'd spent the weekend looking at myself in the mirror and thinking, Now what did you want to go and do that for? The thought kept coming out in my mother's voice.

I was checking out my reflection in the bowl of my spoon when I noticed this guy in the next booth. He was talking to himself and maybe that's what I noticed first, or maybe it was that he was good looking and alone, or maybe it was the streak of white in his hair that made me think of Holden Caulfield. The Chinese waiter, coffee pot in one hand and menus in the other, kept passing by Holden, who would stare forlornly after him. I picked out his voice from the background clatter of the cafe, and he was saying: "May I have a cup of coffee, please?" He kept shifting the emphasis from word to word like an actor rehearsing a line. I picked up my coffee cup and slid into the seat across from him. I held up my cup and the waiter came and gave us both refills.

"Thanks," said Holden and smiled. A rueful, little boy smile. God save me from the little boy men.

His real name was Homer. He had to tell me three times before I believed him.

When I woke up in the morning it was with his arm beneath my head. He was awake and smiling at me.

"I can't sleep in strange places," he said.

It was nice to wake up with somebody again. Even when I was with Tom he hardly ever stayed straight through until morning. I wasn't over Tom though, and the way I could tell was I kept looking for the ways that Homer's body differed from his. Tom was a big, solid man and Homer was built more like me, skinny and sparrow-boned.

"I'll get breakfast," Homer said. "You stay right where you are." He pulled on his clothes and backed out of the bedroom. I thought I'd died and gone to heaven until I heard the slam of the front door. Well, that's that, I thought. Nothing sloppy or sentimental about that one.

An hour later he showed up with two suitcases.

"Back into bed," he said. "You weren't supposed to move." He dumped the contents of one of the suitcases onto my bed, spilling out an assortment of stuffed animals and an espresso maker. He stashed the espresso maker under his arm and headed for the kitchen. I grabbed a penguin that had landed near my feet and nestled under the covers with it.

"Make yourself at home," I told it.

3.

The first thing Leila asked me at lunch the next day was why in the hell I had dyed my hair red.

"I was depressed," I said. "I thought it might cheer me up."

"Well, I don't like it, you don't look like you anymore."

"I think that was the general idea," I said.

Leila and I both worked for the same corporation and we had lunch together every day. This was looked on with suspicion and disapproval by our co-workers because Leila was middle management while I was a lowly clerk-steno. I didn't mind being shunned by the other clerk-stenos though because I'd found them to be a pretty narrow-minded lot. I was never able to hold up my end of the conversation when it came to things like recipes for light morning coffee cake.

"So who's the new guy?" Leila asked.

"How do you know there is one?"

"You've got that way of moving back again, like your bones are made of jello or something. You're only that way when you're getting it."

"You're right," I said. "There might be somebody new but it's still too early to tell."

Leila was my best friend in the whole world, but I didn't know how to tell her that a week after the supposed love of my life had walked out on me I had taken up with an out-of-work actor named Homer. Leila has a house and a husband and all those things that everybody is supposed to want.

"Fine," she said. "Don't tell me who he is then. I just hope he's helping you get over that shit Tom. No lectures, I promise. Just tell me you're happy."

"You know how in movies, love stories I mean, there's always that scene midway through where it's all holding hands and smiling at the balloon man in the park and all that hokey stuff? Where about a week passes in three minutes and everything's happening real fast and in time with horribly significant background music?"

"Yeah," said Leila. "The one that's the MTV version of your life, or maybe somebody else's life."

"Right," I said. "That's what I'm waiting for."

"Poor baby," she said. "You really want it all, don't you?"

4.

Homer never went home again after that first morning; he became just another part of my daily routine very quickly. He would be up before I was in the morning and I would wake to the smell of coffee brewing, and when I got home at the end of a day dinner would be on the table. It was like having a wife.

About a week after he came to stay I got home from work one day and there was no dinner on the table. Homer was sitting in the dark on the couch, pouting.

"You got a letter today," he said and handed me a postcard. It was one of those gag cards where instead of a picture it's just black and at the bottom it says in white lettering: *Toronto at night.* On the back was scrawled: *Wish you were here.*

"Must be somebody's idea of a joke," I said to Homer. I threw it in the garbage and went to sit beside him on the couch.

"Quit your job," Homer said. "You shouldn't be typing somebody's crummy letters all day long. You were meant to lie on a chaise lounge and have somebody feed you grapes. How can you stoop so low as to be a goddamn secretary?"

"It pays the rent," I said.

"Quit. Come away with me. We could go anywhere; we could be anybody."

"Slow down," I said. "We've only known each other a week. What makes you think you know me?"

"Well," he looked around the room. "You love old things. Some people might even call it junk."

I hit him with a pillow embroidered with the slogan: *Souvenir of Niagara Falls.*

"But I like this place," he said. "It feels like a home, like somebody real lives here. Now that — " He pointed to an empty picture frame hanging on the wall. "It makes a statement about art, about minimalism, about the human condition — "

"It's an empty picture frame. I didn't like the picture so I threw it away."

I moved into his lap and pressed my face into his neck.

"Have you ever thought of growing a beard?" I asked.

When Homer was asleep I snuck into the kitchen and rummaged through the garbage until I found the postcard. Bits of potato peels and coffee grounds were stuck to it.

I had to go through all the cupboards to find my teapot. Homer only drank espresso so that was what I'd been drinking too.

The kitchen window reflected myself back at me, shutting out the night. I was paler than usual and my newly-dyed red hair made me look freaky.

The card was postmarked Toronto.

He missed me.

But not enough to give a return address.

5.

I never knew what Homer did in the hours when I was at work and I never really questioned it either. He was like the fridge light: you shut the door and assumed it went out but you never really knew for sure. Homer was one of those people who never gave any sign of having a past; he simply appeared when I needed him.

His life was contained in the second suitcase that sat at the foot of my bed where he'd dropped it the morning he made me breakfast. Things appeared from it and disappeared back into it for the first week or so. Then, one morning before I went to work I emptied a bureau drawer and cleared out some space in the closet. When I got home the suitcase was gone, and neither of us said anything about it. This was as close as we could come to commitment.

Then, just when life was starting to seem normal the call finally came.

"I miss you," he said, before even saying my name.

He just assumed I would answer the phone, that there wouldn't be anybody else here. What if Homer had answered?

"Ruth? Are you there?" he asked when I didn't answer.

"Yes," I said. "I'm here. Where are you?"

"Toronto," he said. "Will you come?"

"The next plane." He gave me the name of a hotel to meet him at.

"Bye luv," he said, and hung up before I could say anything or ask any of the wrong questions.

Homer came home with take-out Chinese while I was packing. I'd sort of forgotten about him and hadn't thought up anything to say to him. He just looked at me like I was someone he didn't know and then set the food down on the bureau and started to help me fold my clothes.

"How long will you be gone?" he asked. Not where, not who with.

"I'm not sure," I said.

He put the last of my clothes into the suitcase and shut it. His lips were tight as he snapped the locks.

"I can drive you to the airport," he said.

"I already called a cab. Thanks."

"You're shaking," he said and drew me to him. He held me tight against his chest until my breath started to slow. He pulled back a little then, so that I had to look at him. "Do you want me here when you get back?" he asked.

"Yes," I said. Then: "It's up to you."

6.

I knew that Tom wouldn't be there to meet my plane but I caught myself scanning the crowds for the silly hat he wore season after season. He wasn't there of course.

The girl who'd shared a seat with me on the plane, and who had occupied her time painting her nails a putrid shade of peach, was now waving her hands frantically in the air. Then above the heads of the crowd I saw an answering pair of waving hands. A man pushed through the crowd, scooped her up like a child and swung her gleefully through the air. Her skirt swirled about, up and over her head and when her face re-emerged she was laughing, almost crying.

They stood there holding hands while the luggage circled past them and every so often she would look up at him as if amazed that he was still there.

I grabbed my suitcase and fled to the nearest washroom. I ran the water as cold as I could get it and then splashed it all over my face, drenching my clothes in the process. My

mascara ran down my cheeks and my hair clung to my face
like seaweed. The face I'd so carefully put on for Tom was
gone. My makeup was in my purse, and I could have started
over, but instead I scrubbed my face dry with a paper towel
until it was red and chapped.

I caught the bus that was going downtown to the hotels
and was suddenly afraid that I'd got the name of the hotel
wrong. Every time the driver would call out a stop I would run
the name over in my mind to see if it sounded familiar. Finally
he called out one that I was sure of and I got off.

When I got into the hotel I realized I didn't know whose
name we'd be booked under. The first thing I did was to head
for the gift shop and buy a pack of cigarettes. I hadn't smoked
for nearly three years but it seemed a good time to start.

I sat down on one of the plush lobby couches and lit a
cigarette to help me think. I watched the people spinning
through the revolving doors: lots of people in swanky clothes
whizzed by, all of them obviously with a set destination. This
was not a hotel for strays and wanderers.

I butted out my cigarette and strode purposefully over to
the desk. Anyone watching me would think I knew where I
was going.

"I have a reservation," I said to the desk clerk. "I believe
the name is Armstrong," I said in a slightly firmer voice. He
looked at me strangely but keyed the name into his computer
and then smiled at me.

"Is your husband with you, Mrs. Armstrong?"

"He'll be joining me later," I said, and took the paper he
shoved across the desk to me. *Mrs. Armstrong*, I signed in a
peculiar backslant. I finished the signature with a flourish that

was supposed to underscore the name but ended up cutting
cleanly through it.

7.

Once I got in the room I found that I couldn't sit down. I put
my suitcase at the foot of the bed and looking at it there made
me think of Homer. I pulled back the drapes, forced the
windows open and looked out on the street: more strangers
whizzing by. Lots of men in hats, but none of them were Tom.

I kept emptying ashtrays so that when he arrived he
wouldn't think I'd been chain smoking, pacing and worrying,
which was exactly what I was doing. I thought of leaving and
coming back; I thought of leaving and not coming back. I
thought of taking off all my clothes and crawling between the
sheets of one of the two neatly turned-down beds, but couldn't
bear the thought of lying there naked and waiting if he wasn't
going to come, and then getting out of bed, putting all my
clothes back on and going home. Or worse, falling asleep and
waking to a dark and empty room.

I perched myself on the window sill, the radiator below
warming me and the cold breeze stinging my face. I searched
the windows of the opposite wing for another face looking
back at me, but there wasn't one. Most of the curtains were
closed and there was no telling what was going on behind
them: who was being loved, who was watching TV, who was
waiting.

Maybe he's dead, I thought. Who'd ever call and tell me;
nobody even knew I was here. Silly. I was getting silly and
maudlin and stupid, alone in this room where I couldn't sit still

for fear of becoming part of the furniture. I was afraid to go
anywhere in case he called and thought I'd changed my mind.
I picked up the telephone receiver to be sure there was a dial
tone.

I had to go to the bathroom, but couldn't because I didn't
want him to arrive while I was sitting on the toilet. I didn't want
day-to-day details intruding on what should be magic.

I thought of the couple in the airport again. There was
nothing out of the ordinary about them. Nothing magic. Except
for the pure joy I had found myself standing on the periphery
of. They'd get old together, eventually he'd take to calling her
Mother, as in: *How about another cup of tea, Mother?* She'd take
to calling him the old fart and complaining when he cut his
toenails in bed. And maybe they'd forget that scene in the airport
long before I would, but it would always be with them. His
arms lifting her higher and higher into the air.

I started to cry all over again, and decided that was it, I
would go to the airport and stay there until they could get me
a flight home. I was in the bathroom when I heard the key turn
in the lock.

8.

I found that I couldn't sleep beside him and when I turned
toward him, his body moved away from mine.

I pulled the blanket off the second bed and curled myself
into a ball on the armchair and watched the city lights outside
the window. It was getting harder and harder to breathe in the
small room even with the window open. I dug through Tom's
overnight bag until I found the bottle I knew would be there.

I went to the bathroom for a glass, trailing my blanket behind me as though it was the train of some grand wedding gown.

I poured myself a good stiff shot and raised my glass in a toast to Tom's sleeping form. "It's a helluva long way to come for a lay," I said. His eyelids didn't even flicker. I grabbed the phone book off the desk and dropped it on the floor. Thud. Nothing. So then I picked up the phone and dropped it too. Thud-jangle. And still nothing.

I placed the phone back on the desk and thought about who I could call. I didn't know anybody in this city except an old boyfriend whom I didn't expect would be too happy to hear from me. And then I thought of Tom's wife, sleeping somewhere in the city alone, but I couldn't think of her and breathe at the same time.

I dialed my own number and let it ring once before I hung up. I didn't want to think of Homer in my apartment waiting for me, and even worse was the thought of the apartment empty waiting for my return.

I slipped out of my blanket and climbed up on the windowsill and pressed my naked body up against the glass. When my body was cold and I couldn't hold back the shivers any longer I pulled back the covers and lay my body over Tom's, drawing the warmth from him. When he opened his eyes the first thing I said was: "Talk to me."

"Hello, other world," he said, and I licked his face with my whisky tongue.

When I woke up he was gone. Even though I'd known he was going I'd expected him to stay, to change his mind. To choose me.

9.

Homer was waiting for me when I got home.

"I thought you would have gone," I said.

"Thought or hoped?" he asked. He was sitting on the couch, in the dark, naked except for a pair of plaid bedroom slippers that I'd never seen before.

"Don't be silly," I said. "I'm glad you're here. Really."

"I tried to leave, I truly did. I even went home but the other guys had rented out my room and all my plants had died." He pointed to the corner and I saw the skeleton of a fig tree in a huge pot.

"I like it," I said. "It's very minimalist. It makes a statement about — "

"I missed you," he said. "I tried not to, but I did."

"Come talk to me while I unpack," I said. He followed me into the bedroom, walking so close behind me that I could feel his breath on the back of my neck.

"Is it over?" he asked.

"I don't know."

10.

Leila phoned first thing the next morning to tell me not to bother coming in to work if I was even thinking about it; they'd canned me when I didn't show up Monday without calling in.

I promised to meet her at the bar when she got off work and answer all her questions.

"Homer," I called, after hanging up the phone. He was sleeping on the couch. He'd gotten up in the middle of the night and said sorry, but he couldn't sleep with me when I smelled of somebody else.

"Homer," I yelled again. I lit a cigarette and coughed. "I can be anybody now," I said, but there was no answer.

I lay in bed for a long time, my body just a solid mass beneath the covers. I concentrated on removing myself from my body, trying to float a few inches above myself the way they say dying people do. For a moment I made it: I could see myself lying there swaddled in sheets as if I was a newborn. And then I was back. I stayed lying there; it seemed the best thing to do as there was nowhere to go.

Finally I got up because I thought I could smell coffee brewing. Homer wasn't on the couch, or in the kitchen, or anywhere else in the apartment. There wasn't any coffee either.

I was still in bed at six o'clock that night when the security buzzer went. At first I thought it was the alarm clock and it was time to get up for work. It was Leila and she was mad as hell.

When I let her in she said: "Christ, Ruth, you look like shit," and pushed past me into the living room.

"Where'd you get the twig in a pot?" she asked, pointing at Homer's dead fig tree. "And where the hell have you been? And why didn't you meet me in the bar when you said you would? And who is this Homer guy whose been answering your phone? Is he for real?" She didn't wait for answers, just stormed past me into the kitchen and started banging the cupboard doors.

"Where the hell's the coffee pot?" she yelled at me when I followed her into the kitchen. Bang, bang, crash. "I'm drunk by the way. I had three lousy Manhattans sitting in the bar by myself, getting eyed by all the leisure suits. Oh here it is." She dumped in some grounds, plugged it in and then sat down, gesturing at me to do the same.

"Why'd you do it?" she asked. "Why'd you go back to him?"

"I didn't mean to," I said. "Really, I didn't want to. I just did it."

"What's in it for you? Where's the thrill?" Leila got up again and unplugged the coffee pot. "I changed my mind," she said, and began banging the cupboards again.

"Under the sink," I said.

"Ah." She pulled out a half-empty bottle of scotch, left over from the days of Tom. "Serious business here." She poured out two shots, heavy on mine, and then sat down again. "You know," she said. "I've always wanted to love a man to the point of losing all control. To the point of insanity."

I got up and opened a cupboard and pulled out a cast iron skillet. "You see this thing?" I asked brandishing it at her. "My mother gave it to me when I got my first apartment; I think she must have gotten it as a wedding present, it's that old. I've never cooked anything in this damn pan, but I'm saving it. You know why?"

Leila just shook her head and took a pull off her drink.

"I'm saving it because someday there's going to be a man that I love enough to hate enough and then I'm going to throw the damn thing at him."

Leila just stared at me for a minute and then she started to laugh, rich deep waves of laughter that ended in snorts and gasps for air. I laughed too, until the tears came.

11.

Tom had given me his number. "When am I ever going to use this?" I'd asked and he'd laughed, but it was a raw sound.

I'd kept the number, and one lonely night about a week after Homer did his vanishing act I found myself dialing it. I told myself that if Jacquie answered then I would hang up. It would be like a sign. But when she said hello, her voice thin across the wire, I felt a weird fascination. This was the woman with the red hair, the one that Tom went home to, the one who had it all.

We both listened to the silence and then she said: "I know who you are," real quiet and deadly. "I know all about you." Hang up, I thought, but I couldn't do it. "You really think you're something, don't you?" she said. "You really think . . . "

I placed the receiver down on the floor with her voice still spilling out of it and backed out of the room.

I took a bath. I was out of bubble bath so I used the dish soap and it made nice fat bubbles that you could see the world in, upside down.

12.

Homer came home again. He snuck in while I was asleep and was in bed beside me when I woke. I guess I'd been expecting him back. "I went to the Starlight," he said. "Someone took me home. I wanted to hurt you. I didn't want you to go."

"I know," I said, fitting my body to his.

While he was loving me, my eyes were open and I was watching the moon outside my window, and wondering, if I could see the moon, could the moon see me?

THE GAZEBO STORY

There were these two kids . . . call them Frankie and Johnny, those names are as good as any. They were in love these two, or leastwise moving in that direction, against all probability too, having been friends so long as to have very few secrets with which to weave an aura of mystery. If I were a person of no small generosity I would leave them here, both forever young and forever on the very verge of falling. But to get on with the story: they had planned a secret rendezvous. They were to meet in Saskatoon in the riverside park at midnight.

Split screen: he on a highway driving north and she on a different highway driving south. Cut to a wide-angle shot of Saskatoon and zoom in on the park and the gazebo. White, glowing, and not really a gazebo at all, but a bandstand. The Vimy Memorial to be precise. Problems of terminology already arising. Cut to the gazebo at the other end of the park.

Frankie is wearing white — she is the kind of girl who can get away with that sort of thing. Smear a little vaseline on

the lens and think of Lillian Gish, get the picture? She is carrying
a basket (wicker) with wine and flowers (violets) and a blanket.
Think of fairy tales, think of little red. Think of the wolf.

Frankie is in the park now, but she has lost her way. She
is from a small town: this is important — perhaps I should have
mentioned it sooner. She sees the gazebo but no Johnny; there
are a couple of guys necking on a bench and she approaches
them. "Looking for Johnny?" they ask. "Yes," she says. "I am."
She has always wondered about men with other men and how
the parts fit together and don't fit together, but doesn't suppose
this is the time to ask. "Have you seen him?" she asks. "He went
that way," they tell her, and point in the direction she has just
come from. "Thank you," she says, and inexplicably curtseys.
Even she doesn't know why she does it, something to do with
the dress, the moon.

Insert some stock footage of the moon here. A lover's
moon. A werewolf's moon. The kind that is so round and sharp
it looks like it was pasted onto the backdrop of sky. Keep it
short, we don't want to get hackneyed.

Johnny is wearing a rented tux; it was expensive but he
figures it will be worth it when he sees the look on Frankie's
face. Johnny looks a little like James Dean. Give him a pout
and a red windbreaker and you'd have it. It's hard to get Johnny
to pout though, he grins too readily. If Jimmy Dean had smiled
this much he probably would be an old man today.

Johnny is at the bandstand now; he's worried about his girl. He likes saying it like that: my girl. He is sitting on the steps with his ghetto blaster loaded up with Bobby Darin. He plays "Mac the Knife" over and over and thinks of himself as a sort of lighthouse. He has been propositioned three times in the last hour, twice by women, and once he was tempted. He likes the fact that he was tempted because otherwise there's no virtue in saying no.

Get a good shot of the park here. Track the camera along the lighted trail that runs from the gazebo at one end to the bandstand at the other. Outside the light of the path you can see scattered benches, park denizens, and even a fountain. Maybe later we can get a shot of someone dancing in the fountain. Maybe not.

Frankie has met some real nice people in the park and most have warned her that she shouldn't be out so late, dressed in white and all. She knows she is safe and it is this knowing that seems to protect her. She's talked to lots of people who've seen Johnny sometime tonight. You two would make a real cute couple, they tell her. They organize search parties but by the time they return with Johnny, Frankie has moved on.

The people who inhabit the park at night are the kind you never see during the day, or if you do then you probably cross over to the other side of the street. These people should be shot only in partial light: let them slip golem-like in and out of the shadows.

Johnny is approached by a guy decked out in leathers and chains. The guy definitely doesn't look like a Bobby Darin fan, and Johnny is thinking to himself: oh shit. "You Johnny?" the guy asks. Johnny is thinking: am I Johnny? Will it help me to be Johnny? "Yeah," he says. "I'm Johnny." He is thinking: if you get hit don't bleed on the tuxedo. "Frankie's been looking all over for you, man. What the hell are you doing here? You're supposed to be at the gazebo." How's this guy know so much about Frankie? Johnny wonders. "Isn't this the gazebo?" he asks. "No," says the guy. "It's the Vimy-fucking-Memorial." Johnny looks up and sure enough right over the archway it says: Vimy Memorial. "Who's this Vimy guy?" he asks.

Hold the shot on the Vimy for a few seconds after Johnny and the other guy walk out of the shot. We should be able to pick up some nice light and shadow play from the moon hitting it through the trees.

Frankie is tired of looking for Johnny and decides that she's missed him, and he's probably given up on her and gone home. She finds a circle of teenagers who look interesting and offers to share her wine with them. She forgot to bring a corkscrew, but luckily one of the guys has a blade strapped to his calf and it does the trick. Frankie has to leave soon; she has to get her mother's car back before morning. She offers a ride home to anyone who wants one, but nobody answers her, they just start to talk about other things real fast. Frankie slowly clues in that they don't have homes to go to. She doesn't think she has ever met a homeless person before; there weren't any in the town she came from.

Pull back for a wide angle of the park: the gazebo at one end and the bandstand/memorial at the other. Somewhere in the middle is the old hotel that looks like a castle. Be sure the moon makes it into the shot.

Johnny makes his way through the park to the gazebo. He stands and stares at it for a long time and thinks: so that's what a gazebo is. Frankie isn't there. Nobody's there. Johnny had such plans for this night. He was going to dance with Frankie under the moon. He was going to tell her how he feels about life, about the small town he came from, about her. Anything might have happened. He'll walk through the park once more and if he doesn't find her he will go home. There will be other nights, other moons.

Get a travelling shot of Johnny walking down the path to the bandstand. Just outside the light can be seen silhouettes of people propped up against trees, or fighting, or sitting around drinking. One of these silhouettes belongs to Frankie. Pick up just a hint of her white dress, nothing too obvious.

Frankie finally gives up on trying to give the homeless people rides anywhere, but when she gets up to leave she accidentally on purpose leaves her blanket behind. She gives away her violets saying: "Rosemary, that's for remembrance," the only line she can remember from the high school play she was in. She's trying real hard not to be disappointed about Johnny. Things could always be worse.

Wide angle of the park with the Vimy Memorial more or less centred in the shot. If you can do it try to catch Johnny on one edge of the periphery walking out of the shot while Frankie enters the shot from the other side. Cut to a split screen: he on the highway driving south, and she on another highway heading north. Maybe the other way around.

THE CITY AS SEEN FROM THE AIR

As the plane descended, Eva leaned up against the window to look down, trying first, as she always did, to pick out their house, the house she had lived in for her entire childhood. Once, a few years after she'd moved away to Montreal, her father had the roof re-shingled in a different colour and she'd been disoriented, suddenly unable to recognize the house from the air. Once she'd placed the house, she looked next for the three sisters. When she was growing up there were two houses in her neighbourhood — old solid houses, exact images of each other, that were called the three sisters, even though there were only two of them.

Whenever she remembered Saskatoon or dreamed of it, it was always as it appeared from the air. It was not home she missed, so much as the sense of going home.

༄

It was one o'clock by Saskatoon time but her watch still read eleven. It was eleven o'clock in Ottawa where the conference representative sent to the airport to meet her would be trying to find out why she wasn't on the flight. It was also eleven o'clock in Montreal, where her family did not yet realize that she had left them.

♨

"How much longer?" asked Annie, sounding more like seven than seventeen.

"You didn't have to come, Annie, you could've stayed in bed until we got back," Meribeth said, and handed the half-empty styrofoam cup of coffee back.

"I wanted to come. Tell me again what she said." Annie was bigger than Meribeth, taller and broader through the shoulders, but she leaned up against her older sister as though she wanted nothing so much as to crawl into her lap and be read a story.

"She just said she needed to get away for awhile."

"Not why?" Annie took a small sip of the coffee, blew on it and took another.

"No, not why. I told you," said Meribeth.

"But why didn't you ask her? How did she sound?"

"She sounded, I don't know, tired. Far away," said Meribeth.

"Well, she was far away."

"No, you know what I mean. Distant. Annie, what have you got on underneath that coat?"

Annie was wearing her mother's old muskrat coat and fleece boots that went up to her knees. She undid the top few buttons of the coat and showed Meribeth her plaid flannel pyjamas.

"Oh, Annie," Meribeth said, and she made the face her mother would've made had she been there, a small bemused shake of the head. Annie looked at her older sister and thought how much she looked like their mother, but knew better than to say so.

"Look, they're coming." Annie stood and peered myopically at the disembarking passengers. "Can you see her yet?"

People were starting to exit the upstairs gate and come down the escalator, all of them with the same expression of searching on their faces and then the smile, and sometimes a wave when they found who they were looking for.

"There she is," said Meribeth. "How does she look to you?"

"Far away," said Annie. "You know, distant."

&

When Eva came through the glass doors Meribeth and Annie were standing right there waiting for her but there was a moment when not one of them made a move toward the other. Annie was a little taller than Meribeth but they shared the same wispy blonde hair and grey eyes that came from their mother's side of the family. Eva was darker, and what her mother had always referred to as "heavy-boned" and looked more like her father. They stood, like the three points of a triangle, waiting for someone else to make the first move, to set the tone for this visit. Annie broke first, giving her oldest sister a hug.

"Welcome to Saskatoon, the winter getaway destination of choice," she said and they all laughed, but still the tension did not break and fall away.

&

Driving through Saskatoon Eva was silent, watching the city through her window, noting new buildings that had gone up in her absence and old ones that had disappeared. The city looked flattened and the sky looked large and empty. It was a piercing blue in colour and everything had extra sharp edges from the cold air.

"I've missed hoar frost," she said. "I've only just realized."

Both of her sisters nodded seriously, as though she had actually told them something. As though she had given them a clue to make sense of this situation.

Every small sign of change in the city made Eva feel older, distanced from her childhood and youth. When she'd looked down from the plane it had been as though she were looking at the little toy town that the *Friendly Giant* went walking through in his big, big boots.

"What are you looking at?" asked Meribeth. She didn't take her eyes off the road. She was driving slowly because of the icy roads and Annie could see from the back seat how tightly she was holding on to the steering wheel.

"Oh," said Eva. "Everything looks so strange." She started to explain but stopped herself.

꒰꒱

The phone was ringing when they opened the front door; Annie went running down the hall, her boots dropping slush and mud all over the floor.

"Eva," she shouted from the kitchen. "It's for you."

"I'm not here," Eva shouted back.

Annie came around the corner, with the cordless phone muffled in the fur of her collar.

"But Eva," she said, "it's your husband." She said the word *husband* with a certain hushed reverence. The truth was that she'd always been a little afraid of Stephen because she could never tell when he was joking and when he wasn't. He said everything with the same tone of faintly amused boredom, and Annie and Meribeth had decided between them that he found their whole family slightly quaint and provincial, a word that was not theirs but his.

"I'm not here," Eva repeated. She took off her coat and threw it over the bannister.

Annie looked at her, and then looked to Meribeth as though waiting for instructions. Meribeth shrugged, but not enough so that Eva would notice.

"Um, Stephen, Eva's not here, okay. Kiss my nefs for me." She listened to him say something and shook her head. "I've really got to go. Sorry. Bye." She pushed down the disconnect button on the phone and stood there holding it. "What's going on Eva? Stephen asked if you seemed normal. What does he mean?"

"It doesn't mean anything, sweetie. Don't worry about it."

"But Eva, it doesn't make any sense. Why did you say you weren't here? Why are you here?"

Meribeth went over and took the phone from Annie. "Don't be foolish," she said. "It's Eva's home as much as yours or mine." While her back was to Eva she made a small shushing noise at Annie. Then she turned around and smiled at Eva. "Pancakes sound good?" she asked.

৯

While Annie was making the pancakes, Meribeth put coffee on and Eva sat down at the kitchen table and lit a cigarette.

"I thought you quit," Meribeth said.

"I did," said Eva.

"Lucky Mom's not here to see you," said Annie without turning from the counter where she was measuring and sifting. "She'd have a bird."

"How are they?" Eva asked. "Have you heard?"

Meribeth took a postcard off the fridge and gave it to Eva. It had a picture of the Tower of London on the front, and a message in their mother's handwriting on the back. Eva scanned it and then put it down on the table.

"Have you ever noticed," she asked, "how Mother always says *we*? *We* did this, *we* saw such and such, *we* send our love?"

"I guess it's only natural," Meribeth said. "They've been married since forever."

"It gives me the creeps," said Eva.

Meribeth and Annie exchanged a look, a look that said: *now what do you suppose that's all about?*

"Here," said Eva. "Give me the apples, Annie, and I'll chop them for you."

"No," said Annie, "You don't get to do anything. You just sit there and let us wait on you."

"Why?" asked Eva, "it's not my birthday or anything."

"No, but . . . " Annie trailed off. She was thinking: *but there's something wrong and I don't know what it is.* She thought of her oldest sister as a grown-up, an almost mythical creature. There was twelve years difference in their age, Annie being the family's little afterthought. Eva wasn't the same as their parents but she was somebody's mother after all.

"So the kids are okay?" asked Meribeth, sitting down to the table with Eva. Meribeth loved her nephews fiercely, unlike Annie who loved them when they were in range and forgot about them the rest of the time. When Annie bought them

Christmas presents they were always for children either younger
or older than the boys actually were. She wasn't aware of them
in the same way Meribeth was.

"Fine."

Meribeth waited but Eva didn't say anything more. "And
Stephen?" she asked.

"He's fine." Actually, thought Eva, that's exactly the right
word for Stephen. Fine: like weather that was neither terribly
good nor terribly bad. An ordinary, fine day.

She smiled without knowing it, leaving Meribeth to ponder
her expression.

"So . . . ?" asked Meribeth.

"So, what's the problem, you mean?"

"Yeah, I guess. I mean, you don't have to say if you don't
want to."

"I just don't know. Everything's fine. Everything except
me. Or maybe I'm fine too. Maybe I'm just tired of being fine."
Eva got up and left the kitchen. From the hallway she shouted
back: "Maybe I'm in the mood for a storm."

ᴥ

All that week, Eva hardly left the house at all. Annie was at
high school doing her mid-terms; Meribeth was at the university
researching a paper she was writing for a journal. Annie would
come home from classes at lunch time and Eva would be just
getting up, and they'd sit in the kitchen together and eat grilled
cheese sandwiches and tomato soup. It was the same thing
every day. It was a small, safe world.

"Don't you ever get tired of this?" Eva asked.

"Tired of what?" Annie asked.

"The same food over and over; it's Friday today and we've had the same thing every day this week."

"Oh," said Annie. "I could make you something else if you like."

"No, it doesn't matter. I just mean, don't you ever want something else? Don't you ever want tuna fish sandwiches and cream of celery soup?"

"No," said Annie. "This is what I always have. I've been eating it since I was a kid."

"You are a kid," said Eva.

"No, I'm not. I'm graduating this spring, and — "

"Yeah, but you'll always be a kid to me," said Eva. "Do you know what the funny thing about this kitchen is?" She stood up and looked out the window over the sink and into the backyard. The snow was deep and so crisp that it still showed the holes where their feet had sunk through as they walked from the garage the day that she arrived.

"Funny?" asked Annie, and she looked around the kitchen and then back to Eva and shook her head.

"This kitchen," said Eva, "is the only place in the world where I feel tall. I always expect to have to reach up for things that I don't — getting things out of the freezer, washing the dishes and putting the plates away, looking out the window — and it seems all wrong somehow. Does that make any sense?"

"No," said Annie, "not really."

"No, I didn't suppose it would. But just wait, your time will come. Once you leave everything changes on you. It's as though everything and everybody just expands to fill the space you've left behind you."

"You just said things were smaller and now they're bigger. Which is it?" Annie asked without expecting any decent answer.

"Neither. Everything's just the same only now it gives me vertigo."

❧

Annie came home late from a date with Jerry and found Eva, dressed in one of their mother's matching polyester nightgowns and robes, tearing through the closet of the spare room. Annie stood in the doorway, unseen by Eva, and thought briefly that her sister must be drunk.

Eva was pulling papers, books and objects from boxes and throwing them out into the centre of the room where they lay, scattered and broken in a messy heap. Boxes lay tipped and useless at her feet.

"You okay?" asked Annie.

Eva whipped around, cracking her head on the door frame of the closet as she did so. "Christ," she said. "Didn't your mother ever teach you not to sneak up on people?"

"Are you looking for something?" asked Annie. She wondered where Meribeth was, if she should go and get her to calm Eva down. Eva laughed. It was an ugly sound as though she had forgotten how. She stepped out into the middle of the room and stood by the heap of her old possessions.

"Why did she save all this stuff?" Eva asked, pushing at it with a bare toe.

"I don't know. I guess she thought you might want it some day." Annie was slowly backing out of the room, wishing she hadn't come home, hadn't been witness to this. At the same time, she felt that this would be the moment to ask Eva a question — that the answer given would be an honest one. But she couldn't begin to think what question to ask.

Eva picked up a black hardbound notebook and opened it randomly. As a morbid sixteen year old she had poured all of her turbulent emotions and desires onto these pages. Now, looking at them, she thought they might as well be written in code for all they signified to her.

"Do you know who you want to be?" Eva asked her sister. "not what, but who?"

"Eva," said Annie, holding on to the door frame, "you're scaring me. Please stop."

❖

Eva refused to take Stephen's calls, but during the day when she knew he was at work and Ben and Luke off at school she would phone and leave messages for the boys on the machine, motherly things she thought she should be worried about: *Brush your teeth*, she would say after the beep. *Be good for your father while I'm away.* Really though, she wasn't concerned about them, or at least no more so than usual. She knew that Stephen would take good care of them.

Eva didn't tell her sisters about these daytime calls, and when they asked her if she didn't miss her children she said, "Of course I do. What do you think I am? A monster?" It was a question that she asked herself over and over in the small hours of the night. She didn't feel remorse about leaving. She didn't miss any of them; all she felt was a quiet and profound relief.

She didn't leave any messages for Stephen. She didn't know what to tell him.

&

On Saturday night all three sisters went out for supper; Eva didn't want to at first, but Meribeth insisted, and Annie said that she wanted to go to the new French restaurant downtown because she thought she could get served drinks there and besides she and Meribeth could wear the dresses Eva had sent them for Christmas from Laura Ashley's in Montreal. They were velvet; Meribeth's was blue and Annie's was green. They both got dressed and then went into their parents' room where Eva was, to show her. They stood and admired themselves in the big mirror over their parents' maple bureau.

The dresses were all wrong, were too young, too girlish and Eva realized this as soon as she saw her sisters wearing them. She wondered what she had been thinking and why she had bought them matching outfits as though she'd been shopping for children.

"Look," said Annie, "we look like bridesmaids." And then she fell silent because she was remembering that the only time they had been bridesmaids together had been at Eva's wedding, when Annie was ten and Meribeth was seventeen. Meribeth had spent the entire evening trying to catch the eye of the best man who spent all of his time dancing with Annie, her shoeless feet placed on his tuxedo pumps as he swirled her round and round.

"Sorry, Eva," said Annie. "I didn't mean . . . "

"It's okay, I mean it's not as if I've been widowed or anything. I'm not even sure if I've really left him or not."

"You'll go back to him," said Meribeth. "Of course you will." She said it like she believed it. Perhaps she did.

"I might go back," said Eva with a deliberately light tone. "Then again, I might not."

They had two cocktails each in the lounge before they went in for dinner. Annie asked for a drink menu and read over all the names, trying to decide what she wanted. She decided, first, on a Tom Collins, but Meribeth said that Mother said you never drank gin after Labour Day. It was like white shoes. Eva told Annie she could have whatever she wanted, so she had a Tom Collins and then a Brandy Alexander. Meribeth had white rum and coke, both times, and Annie accused her of being a stick in the mud. Eva had two glasses of Dubonnet and looked at her sisters thinking how she'd always been so much older than they and wondering what it would have been like if they'd been closer.

Eva ordered a bottle of wine to go with supper, and then another when they finished the first one. She wasn't sure if she was trying to get drunk, or if she just liked the sight of her sisters' faces getting rosier and rosier by the candlelight. They looked young, both of them; they looked like children. They looked, Eva realized, like her own children: the same colour of hair and eyes, the same heart-shaped faces.

ﻋ

When Luke was born, Eva had been embarrassed by the surges of love that she felt for him. As though it had never happened to anybody else. He wasn't what she expected somehow — throughout her pregnancy when she had tried to picture her child or found himself dreaming of him he had always either a face that was a composite of Stephen's and her own, or else a face that was completely that of a stranger. But when she looked at him for the first time, his clear blue eyes looking straight back into her own, she had been shocked by the overwhelming feeling that he was just completely himself.

Then, sixteen months later when Ben had arrived, she had gone through it all again, the shock of falling in love with someone you felt you had always known.

&

Annie was talking about graduation now. She was going with a boy she'd been seeing, off and on, since grade ten. He was a nice boy, his name was Jerry, and he was at ease in the family, almost one of them. Everyone expected that they would marry some day, but Eva had the feeling it meant more to their mother than it did to Annie.

"I'm thinking," said Annie, "of going to Australia after grad. Lisa — you remember Lisa, don't you? — wants to go, too. She has an uncle in Melbourne who will let us work in his hotel."

"As chambermaids," said Meribeth, with a note of disapproval.

"Yes," said Annie, "as chambermaids, but that's okay. It's not forever. I haven't told Mom yet — I'm waiting until after her trip."

The waiter came round and poured the last of the wine into their glasses and took the empty bottle away. Annie raised her glass to make a toast, and then hesitated trying to think of something to say.

"To sisters," she said, and they all repeated it and drank to each other and themselves.

"You two, you both have your whole lives ahead of you," said Eva. She was immediately sorry she'd said it; it sounded like something a maudlin spinster aunt would say, but the sisters just laughed. Eva looked at them, the colour high in their faces, the space around them as still and composed as a painting, and she thought, but did not say, you are as beautiful as you will ever be.

❧

When they came home from the restaurant that night Eva announced she was going to sleep in her parents' bed.

"I'm having a terrible time sleeping," she said.

Eva slept dead in the centre of the bed so that she was neither on her mother's side of the bed nor on her father's.

She dreamt that she and Stephen were living in the same apartment but everything was different. There was no sign of Ben and Luke anywhere. There were none of their toys or books lying on the floor. She wandered from room to room looking for proof of their existence but there was none to be found. In the last room, the study, she found Stephen sitting alone. "Looking for something?" he asked.

❧

For several months before she left Stephen, Eva had been suffering from insomnia. She had started leaving a change of clothes in the bathroom and in the middle of the night, when Stephen and the boys were all asleep, she would get up, creep to the bathroom and put her clothes on, and sneak out of the apartment. She would go for walks, long aimless walks around the neighbourhood. Down along Jeanne Mance Park, with Mount Royal looming on her left, or sometimes over to the Main where people would be coming and going from bars and cafés, sometimes all the way up to Fairmount, where she'd buy a fresh bagel to warm her up. She'd stand inside the bagel factory to eat, gazing through to where the graveyard shift bakers fed the long paddles into the flames of the great stone ovens. She loved to watch them working the dough for the bagels, the dexterity of their movements, as though they were doing just exactly what they should be.

Sometimes she would stop and have a coffee or a drink but usually she just walked. She never talked to anyone, and people mostly left her alone. What she liked best was to walk down the street looking in windows where there were lights on and the blinds were up or curtains were open. She liked to think what type of life would be hers if she lived in that apartment with the calico cat sitting on the window sill and the painting of a naked woman over the fireplace, for example. Or the place with all the plants in the window and the deep mud-coloured couch that looked as if it could swallow you right up and hide you from view. Or the apartment with books lining all three visible walls and no furniture at all, excepting a chair and a lamp. She didn't stop to look into windows where the rooms were peopled, only the empty ones, and whenever she pictured herself in these places she was always alone.

Eva had tried to make Stephen understand that she was unhappy but he'd dismissed it. He put it down to circumstances. He suggested they move, buy a place in the townships, take a holiday without the children.

"You don't understand," she would say.

"You're right," he would say coldly. "I don't understand. Just what is it that you want? What is it that you feel is missing from your life?"

And of course she wouldn't answer. Couldn't answer. And so she had stopped raising the subject. Instead she carried it with her until it turned into a chorus of voices that refused to let her sleep at night, which drove her to circle round and round her own home, trying desperately to exhaust her body so that her mind would have to sleep.

Then, finally, she'd go inside, undress in the bathroom and slide back into bed beside Stephen, being careful not to touch his body with hers until she had warmed up a little. Stephen had never caught on to her secret life and probably wouldn't have if Luke hadn't woken very late at night, delirious with a fever. When she got in, Stephen was sitting in the living room with the lights out, the sleeping child sprawled across his lap.

"Who is it?" he asked Eva when she saw him. "Who have you been with?"

She looked at him, his face white with anger and his jaw clenched so tight he could barely speak.

"Nobody you know," she said.

As soon as she said it she felt a small thrill of something very like revenge.

❧

"Don't you think it's weird?" asked Annie, absent-mindedly stirring her coffee with the end of her pen.

Meribeth and Annie sat at the kitchen table drinking coffee and eating muffins. Annie had made the muffins the night before when she was supposed to be doing her take-home history quiz and now she was trying to finish it in time to leave. Meribeth kept giving her the answers in an involuntary way, like somebody looking over the shoulder of a person doing a crossword puzzle.

"Don't I think what's weird?" asked Meribeth. She wondered how the baby was ever going to make it out in the world alone when it seemed half the time that all her skull contained was loose feathers.

"That she wanted to sleep in the old folk's room. I wouldn't want to sleep in their, you know, marital bed." When Annie was small she had evolved a complicated theory of where babies came from having to do with prayer, rain drops and watermelon seeds. The family only found out about it when she got nearly hysterical after swallowing a watermelon seed at a family picnic.

"Well, the spare room is pretty claustrophobic," said Meribeth. "I wouldn't want to sleep in there — that sloping ceiling always makes me feel that the sky is falling."

"But that's Eva's old room, I mean she slept there right up until she went away to Montreal," said Annie.

"You're going to be late," said Meribeth. "Norman Conquest, Plantagenets, and Katherine of Aragon."

Annie stared blankly at her sister.

"The last three answers," said Meribeth.

ã

When the letter came, as she knew it would, Eva refused to read it. She refused even to touch it. It sat in the centre of the kitchen table where Meribeth had dropped it when she brought the mail in before leaving for work in the morning. All day Annie kept finding excuses to return to the kitchen to see if it was still there. At about two in the afternoon she took a pencil and lightly traced the envelope's outline on the pale yellow oak of the table. When she cleared it away to put down the supper dishes she checked first and saw that it hadn't even been moved all day. The stack of plates in her left hand slammed down against the table and Meribeth jumped, burning her hand on the edge of the soup pot.

"What's got into you?" asked Meribeth.

"I can't take any more of it," said Annie. "It's like she's just slipping into a coma and we're just standing around watching her go. What the hell is wrong with her? Why is she just throwing her life away?"

"Annie," said Meribeth. "I told you. We are not going to interfere."

"Oh, I know what you said, I know. I tell myself over and over all day long. I know that you are the one Daddy always says is the only one of us three with any sense at all, but I can't, I cannot stand it a minute longer." Annie grabbed the letter and ran up the stairs.

Meribeth was standing with her burnt hand under the cold running water when she heard Annie's voice from upstairs. Meribeth couldn't make out what she was saying until she'd reached the landing on the stairs and by then it was too late to stop her.

Annie was standing outside their parents' bedroom door with Stephen's letter in her hand, reading it aloud in a hard voice. The torn envelope lay at her feet. She was shouting through the door so loudly that she didn't hear Meribeth approaching from the stairs.

"Enough," said Meribeth. "That is enough, Annie," and she took the letter from her sister's hand. As soon as she had done so she regretted it because she didn't know what to do with it next. She picked up the envelope from the floor and tried to force the pages back in but they were too crumpled to fit. She smoothed them out with her hand but as she did so words leapt out at her.

The door to their parents' room suddenly opened and Annie and Meribeth were face to face with their sister.

"How dare you?" she raged at both of them, as though they were equally complicit. "It's my life." She ripped the letter and envelope from Meribeth's hands and then the door was slammed against them.

❧

Eva didn't leave her room, her parents' room, the night of the letter. Annie spent most of the evening sitting at the kitchen table, staring at the faint pencilled rectangle on the table's surface, and holding muttered arguments in which she took both parts. Meribeth took her bowl of soup into the living room and ate it in front of the television, something her parents had never allowed, and spent the evening trying to fill her mind with whatever the television could offer. She watched one sit-com after another. Most of them she had never seen before. She didn't know who any of the characters were and she didn't care. The word she most tried not to think of was *abandoned*. Stephen had probably meant the boys, their sons, but in Meribeth's mind the word kept applying to Eva, Eva and her unknown *lover*, and how with him Eva would be a different woman, a woman capable of *abandon*.

❧

The day after the letter, Eva called home and after her own voice invited her to leave a message she began to talk and talk. She said that she needed more time. She told Stephen that there wasn't really anybody else, hadn't ever been anybody else. She told him that she was lonely.

"It frightens me," she said, "how lonely I am when we are together."

When the machine disconnected her she redialed. She told him that she didn't want to write childrens' books anymore, that, in fact, she had never wanted to write childrens' books. She told him that she was afraid of turning into her mother. She told him that she was afraid of wanting too much.

"Maybe I want another child," she said.

She told him she was afraid she didn't want enough. Each time the answering machine cut her off she called back again. She told him that her own reflection in the mirror had been getting dimmer and dimmer. She told him that if the person she was at twenty met the person she was now at a party she wouldn't have anything to say her, wouldn't find her interesting in the slightest. All day long she kept phoning to tell him things she'd just thought of, things she'd never dared to tell him before, things she thought he should know. It was during the course of her monologues into the answering machine, responding to her own recorded voice, that she realized she had begun to picture the apartment, empty, begun to imagine herself there.

"Stephen," she said, and it was the first time since she left that she had spoken his name aloud. "Stephen, I miss you. I miss us all."

And as she set down the phone she was already picturing the city as seen from the air.

INTERIOR

The first I knew of the boy was his clothes, bright flashes of colour spilling down the face of the old seminary. It was the colour that drew my eye, made me press my face up against the glass of the car window to see more. The front of the old seminary had been torn away and I saw a mound of rubble: red bricks, broken floorboards, the crumbled eggshell walls of the interior. Everything muted by a fog of plaster dust. A bathtub had landed in the centre of the front lawn; it sat poised there on its brass claws. And his clothes: flags of faded blue, jade green, and red.

I turned to Jon to see if he had seen it too.

"Didn't I tell you," he asked, "about the demolition? It started the day after you went into hospital. It was all on the news. When they went to start they found that one of the kids who lived there hadn't left. He couldn't because he was dead. He shot himself so full of drugs he must have known he wasn't ever coming down." Jon said all of this looking straight at the road ahead, his eyes refusing to meet mine.

"The body was a full two weeks old when they found it," he said.

That night the boy was walking through the house as we slept. I couldn't hear, but felt him moving from room to room. My pulse was loud enough in my ears to mask the sound of his footfalls, but I knew he was there. My eyes were open but I saw only darkness, not even moonlit shapes. I tried to reach for Jon, but was pressed into the bed by a great weight on my chest. It forced the air from my lungs and water rushed in my ears. I heard my name sounding from a distance and woke in Jon's arms.

"You were dreaming," he said. "It's okay. It's all over now."

In the morning while Jon showered, I walked through the house looking for signs that the boy had been there, but all I found were empty rooms and one door that I couldn't bring myself to open. Jon told me while I was still in the hospital that we would try again as soon as the doctor said we could. He said we would leave the nursery all set up for that time.

"Do you remember when we lived across the street from the old seminary?" Jon asked me as we were eating breakfast. "Some of those kids who got evicted must have been living there then. Maybe even the kid who offed himself."

The old seminary. Forty small rooms, thin walls separating the lives of those who lived there. I wanted to ask about the boy: his name, what he did, how old he was, and other details, but I couldn't ask because I couldn't admit I cared.

"It was a real dead-end place," Jon said.

I pictured them all leaving. Lives packed into suitcases, trunks and boxes. Throwing stained mattresses out the windows

rather than carrying them down the stairs. Tearing posters from
the walls along with strips of faded wallpaper. Stealing the
crystal doorknobs and leaving the doors to swing in the wind.
The boy sleeps through it all.

"Where are you?" asked Jon.

In the bath I saw the boy's naked shape distorting beneath
the water. His veins through milky opaque skin, his eyes
unfocused, his shrivelled penis between razor sharp thighs. The
chipped enamel tub, a mythic beast with clawed feet, cradled
him. It spouted the face of a gargoyle and wings to carry him
away. The tap dripped. Rhythmic as a pulse.

I didn't hear Jon until he was in the room, standing
over me.

"We could've stolen that tub," he said. "You've always
wanted one of those old-fashioned kind."

Jon came into the bedroom to tell me he was leaving for
work and found me swaddled in towels, rocking myself in my
mother's old rocker. I was sobbing, making ugly gasps for air,
but the tears wouldn't come. He got down on his knees and
brushed the hair back off my face.

"Aren't you taking your pills?" he asked.

"I don't want them," I said. "I need to be able to feel."

As I dressed I caught sight of my reflection in the mirror,
my naked flesh, and behind me the crumpled sheets of our
bed, the pillows hollowed by sleep. Then the bed blurred into

a narrow army cot, covered with a coarse red and black plaid blanket. There was a form beneath the blanket, turned away from me. I couldn't see his face.

"Jon," I called, but he was already gone.

I knew that if I turned and reached out my hand the boy would not be there. But I couldn't reach out.

I pulled my dress over my head, the same one I'd taken off the night before. I did not look again at the bed or the mirror, just closed the door softly behind me. I felt the weight of all the rooms of the house pressing down on me and ran down the stairs and out the front door.

I walked past the front gate, past the art gallery and the merry-go-round closed for the season. Riderless horses watched me with crazed glass eyes.

As I crossed the bridge the wind caught hold of my dress and billowed it out in front of me.

Soon I was there, held motionless in front of the old seminary. My hands clutched the wrought iron gate. The trucks and bulldozers stood parked to one side of the lot — work had not yet begun for the day. There were no signs of life.

The tub was gone, as were the clothes I had seen — the flashes of colour. The exposed rooms were bare, barren. At the top of the house where the roof sloped low was a small room with a cot against the far, still-standing wall. I saw the boy, his world closing to four walls and heard the hollow sound of his fists on those walls, trying to beat them back.

He never meant to die, I thought, and suddenly it all came home to me and something broke loose. The poor lost child. And finally the tears. I turned and began the long walk back.

BIG AS LIFE

i. step on a crack

My first memory is of flying. I remember being above the
clouds, with the pressure building inside my head so
that I thought it was growing, inflating like a balloon. I was
pushing back with my head against the cushions of my mother's
breasts, arching with the effort, pushing so hard I was almost
back inside her body. Her arms wrapped around me were
holding me back from my desire to fall out of the round bubble
of the window and into the clouds and the soft white air. My
mother tells me that this is not a true memory, that we were
never on a plane when I was a young child. She tells me that
this memory is most likely something I dreamed once. None of
my memories are true ones and I believe what I choose. My
first memory is of flying.

a.

My mother was on holiday when it happened. Everything
in our family always seemed to happen in the summer. It was
the season when the earth could suddenly shift beneath you,

leaving you breathless in mid-air. She'd gone to Vancouver to give a reading and see some old friends, and while she was there she decided to buy a car. It was, she told me on the phone, the car she'd always dreamed of owning. I never got to see it. I found out later that it had been a white convertible, a VW Rabbit. I never got to see her again. She said on the phone that she was especially looking forward to the mountains.

She was alone in the car when it happened.

ɝ

Apparently Hank was listed on her wallet ID as her next of kin. As far as I knew they hadn't even spoken in years. I wondered if she just hadn't got around to having it changed, or if the choice had been deliberate. If she'd considered the possibility of a stranger calling one of her children to say that something had happened to her. Hank called Stu and Stu called me.

ɝ

She was driving through the mountains when it happened. Apparently she just went off the road. Into the clear blue yonder. She was alone when it happened.

ɝ

The last words my Mother ever said face-to-face to me were: "I never expected any daughter of mine to be boring, Lizzie. I expected a lot of things, but never this." That wasn't really the last thing she ever said, but it was the last real thing.

When I was thirteen years old I began to call my mother Bea. I did it expecting to be rebuked, but I never was. I think it pleased my mother. We were Liz and Bea. We were great chums. We were roommates. We were the same size and could wear each other's clothes if we wanted to, but I didn't want to.

ɞ

My mother and I used to play a card game called *Spite and Malice*. It was a long involved game, like a convoluted double solitaire where you used two decks and played on each other's hand. When we played it would go on for hours. We would sit and smoke and drink tea, and once in a while we would get up to make something to eat and then come back to the game. It always seemed to me to be less a game of skill and more of a test of endurance. It would drag us into the small hours, like two silent beings chained together, and I would remain for the sake of giving my mother the company she needed against the night.

When I was young I thought the game was called *Spike & Alice*, and in the years when my mother and I played it together a series of Alice jokes developed that ran through our daily lives.

"Burnt toast — give it to Alice, she likes it that way."

"Cleaning toilets is Alice work."

Alice was everything my mother wanted me not to be. When I was nervous about anything she would say to me "Let Spike do it." Spike turned into the code word for success, for good news, for achievement. "I Spiked the test." "That was a Spike interview." "Spike strikes again."

With my mother gone I feel more like Alice than ever before.

ॐ

Stu called to tell me that she was gone. The phone rang and
rang and I didn't want to wake up enough to answer it.

"Best?"

"Stuie?"

"Best, I don't know if you know or not, but —"

"Oh, please don't say it." I was whispering.

"Best, it's — "

"Just talk about something else for a minute," I said.

"Best," he said, "I'll be there as soon as I can. I'll meet
you at her house. Will you be alright?"

"No," I said.

ॐ

All the photo albums and everything else from the time we
were a family was lost in the fire when she burned her house
down. I was furious with her for letting the photos be destroyed.
The albums weren't just of our family but also of her parents'
honeymoon in Banff, herself as a bird-legged child, her great-
granny riding a horse, and so on and so forth, back across the
years.

"What does it matter?" she asked me. "They were just
things. We still have each other."

She didn't actually burn the house down, but the fire did
gut it and she lost practically everything. And then her landlord
threatened to sue her. She said it was his fault, because apparently something was wrong with the wiring and she'd been
without power for a few days. This was in the dead of winter.
She'd been using candles to light the rooms at night and the

drapes had caught fire. She was asleep in bed at the time and said she must have forgotten to put out one candle in the living room. She woke up and her room was black with smoke. "I couldn't see anything," she said. "It was like waking up in the belly of a whale."

She made it out of the house safely and called the fire department from the next door neighbour's. A police car dropped her off at my place at three o'clock in the morning. She had on those one-piece long johns like trappers wear, with her fur coat over top. She was clutching her cat, Anon, and an old metal suitcase. When I opened the door to her she started laughing like mad, at me and the look on my face, at herself looking like a bag lady, at the whole mess. "Darling Liz," she said. "You're all I have left in the world. Please take me in."

❧

I have pictures from after Mom and I moved out, ones that I took with me when I moved into my own home. I also have some from the later years, but in those my mother and I stand shoulder to shoulder as adults. Her hair is turning from wheat blond to the silvery ash tone that she had touched up every month. There are no reminders of her as a young woman, or myself as a child, or all of us as a family.

The best likeness I have of my mother is a painting that Hank gave me. It's an abstract, done in plum and amber and burnt orange. The strokes are fierce and sure, and I think it the best thing Hank's ever done. Most people don't even recognize it as a figure, much less a portrait, but I would know my mother anywhere.

ॐ

My mother's house without her in it gave me the same chill as those pictures of Pompeii. Stu was always frightened by pictures of Egyptian tombs and mummies, but they never bothered me in the same way. Those people knew they were going to die. They probably spent their whole lives preparing for it. But the people from Pompeii were different. They were just living their lives right until the end. And still they are the deadest things I ever saw.

I don't think people should be allowed to enter houses where the occupants have died. Such houses should be burned to the ground with everything inside them intact, all their reminders of tasks left forever incomplete: one-armed sweaters, half-eaten pies, shopping lists, library books never to be read.

The house my mother had been living in was a rental, a nice little place on the west side of Saskatoon, close to the riverbank. Before that she had been living in a borrowed cottage on Vancouver Island, writing me letters every week that opened *Darling Liz,* and ended *Best love, Mom.* She came back to Saskatoon about six months before she had her accident. The day she moved into her bungalow by the river she was the happiest I'd seen her in ages. "This feels like a new start," she said. My mother loved new starts better than anything else, I suppose.

This house had a temporary feel to it, as had most of the places she'd lived in on her own since I moved out. She told me once that the older she got the less she needed. She said she was like a woman living in the gondola of a hot air balloon and always worrying that too much excess weight would cause her to lose altitude.

When I opened the door of her house I had to stop myself from calling out to let her know I was there. There was a pile of mail on the floor and that day's paper still stuck in the mail slot, but even that was relatively normal, as if she was just away on one of her trips and I was there to check on the house. As I was picking up the mail the phone started ringing in the bedroom, and I went to answer it thinking it was probably Stu calling to see if I was there yet. I picked up the phone and said hello and a woman's voice on the other end said my mother's name. *Beatrice?* I stood there not saying anything, not knowing what to say — finally I quietly and carefully replaced the receiver, then knelt down and unplugged the phone.

There were things I had to do, preparations to be made — the funeral, the obituary, the clearing out of the house, but I couldn't do any of it. I wanted to be a child again, and in the face of all the responsibility I curled up on my mother's couch with an afghan and went to sleep and didn't wake again until Stu arrived.

When I opened my eyes Stu was standing over me, blocking out the sunlight from the open door so that he was a dark mass outlined in light.

&

Mom stayed with me, in my bachelor apartment, for about three months after the fire and by the end of it we were both suffering our own peculiar variety of cabin fever. She couldn't get used to working her life around my schedule, and in the middle of the night I'd wake up to the sound of the typewriter or Mom singing along with old Ella Fitzgerald records.

"It had to be you," she would sing or, "Let's call the whole thing off," or, "How long I wonder."

They say that people spend about a third of their lives asleep. If most people spend a third of their time sleeping I think with my mother it would have been more like a quarter, or even an eighth. Maybe she knew that her life was going to be a short one, that she would never see the other side of fifty. Maybe by hardly ever sleeping she was trying to balance out the fractions of her life.

Some night I'd get up and talk to her, thinking that she wanted company, but finally I realized she didn't need me at all at those times. She'd be perfectly happy doing crossword puzzles and drinking rye and gingers. She spent most of her time working on her manuscript, trying to remember what happened on the pages from her novel that the fire had claimed. For that was what she had tried to salvage from the fire. Her work. I suppose, now, it makes sense to me but at the time it made me see red. I kept thinking about the baby pictures of Stu, pictures of the three of us from our years at the Lake, family papers, old letters, all the memorabilia of our lives. All of it lost.

&

Stu and I made ourselves a meal from what food there was in the fridge. Everything was approaching its expiry date — it would have to be eaten or thrown away and I couldn't bear to throw it away and so we ate it — ate it all. We made meals like jokes about pregnant women's cravings — pickles and ice cream, salami and crab apple jelly sandwiches.

"Tell me your first memory," I said.

Stu put his feet up on the table. He had one red sock, and one blue.

"The day that man walked on the moon and they showed it on TV."

"That isn't possible," I said. "You weren't even born then."

"Are you sure?" he asked. "Really?"

"Pretty sure," I said. "Almost certain."

"Well, if you say so."

"I remember the day you were born," I said.

"It was raining," he said.

"That's right. There was a tremendous storm. The sky . . . But you can't know that. You can't possibly know that. I must have told you, did I?"

"Probably. You must have."

Stu passed Hagen-Daas chocolate chocolate chip to me. The carton was soggy around the edges at the top and the ice cream had puddles in it, and they looked to me like the lakes on the moon.

"Remember that song she used to sing?" asked Stu.

"Which song?" I asked.

"That song, the one she always sang. About days. You know."

"No," I said. "I don't."

"C'mon, Best. She used to sing that one song all the time."

"What song?"

"The one she used to sing."

"You're making this up. You're trying to drive me mad."

"Short trip."

"Enough out of you."

We were children again, Stu and I.

"I don't think I can eat this," I said.

"Of course you can," Stu said. "Go ahead."

"What did she look like, Stu? Tell me what she looked like. I'm scared to death of forgetting her. I can't imagine anything worse."

"There are worse things," Stu said. "And anyway, you won't forget."

"Tell me anyway."

I got up and closed the living room curtains and pulled the blinds on the kitchen windows.

"She was beautiful like a daisy; a song played on a harpsichord; the northern lights when they crackle; a clean white sheet of paper," said Stu. "She was fierce as an orchid; silent as a tiger; simple as a pomegranate."

We were silent a few moments.

"She wasn't perfect," I said.

"No, she wasn't."

"Didn't you ever resent her?" I asked, watching his face closely. His eyes were as green and unreadable as hers were. "I mean, when she gave you up. Not gave you up, that isn't what I mean — but when she let you stay with Hank, and we moved out."

"I didn't even think about it," he said. "I guess I thought that was how divorces worked. I used to wonder though, what if we had a dog. Who would have gotten the dog?"

"I guess it would have depended on if it were a male or a bitch," I said.

"What about a fish, then," he said, "like a goldfish or one of those black mollies? How do you even tell what those are? How would you know which household it belonged with."

"We would have had to kill it," I said. "Or cut it in half. Is there anything left in the fridge?"

Stu went to look and then came back. "Condiments," he said. "What do we do about the condiments?"

"Condiments don't count," I decided. I was the elder; it fell to me to make such decisions. "We don't have to eat the condiments."

"Those were the days," said Stu.

"What?"

"The song she used to sing. 'Those were the days, my friend'."

"Oh, God, I do remember."

The table was strewn with bits of food and half-emptied jars.

"This is ridiculous," I said. "Why are we doing this?"

"What?"

"Eating."

"I don't know. Because we don't know what else to do, I guess."

ॐ

Stu says that for the longest time when he was a child he was afraid of our mother because he heard her saying something to Hank about killing the angel in the house. He imagined it like a bird trapped in the chimney and our mother going after it with the broom.

I couldn't blame Stu for not recognizing that particular angel, because we very seldom saw her. When Mom discovered writing, she lost all her interest in cookbooks. She told me once that she believed the greatest gift she could offer her children was self-sufficiency.

ða

At the funeral an old woman I didn't know came up to me and said: "I'm so sorry. I didn't even realize she was dying." She obviously hadn't heard about the accident. I didn't know what to say, but Stu spoke up and said: "She wasn't actually, she was living right up until the end." That made me laugh. I tried to hold it back because I didn't want anybody to see me laughing at my mother's funeral, but it kept bubbling out of me in these little choking gasps.

"Go ahead," said Stu. "Laugh. It won't hurt you. Remember what she always said — if you can't laugh, what can you do?"

But I didn't laugh. Instead I cried and let everyone pour sympathy over me like it was going to wash it all away.

ða

When my mother left Hank she didn't have any support system at all. She called her parents from the hospital emergency room to see if we could stay with them, and her mother told her to be sensible and go back to her husband. Then her dad got on the phone and told her to pull herself together. "That's what I'm trying to do," she said and hung up. We ended up renting a crummy apartment with a ceiling that leaked every time the people upstairs had a shower, a stove that only had one element that worked, and painted-shut windows. Mom had been working at the library for a couple years then, but it didn't pay enough for us to live on and so she ended up working as a secretary for a while. She tried not to talk about how much she hated it, but I could tell. What I didn't realize, not until years later, was how afraid she must have been. I think Hank probably would have given her alimony, maybe he even offered, I don't know, but it would have been against her nature to take it. Instead, she invested in a couple of suits and took her typing skills out into the world. It's only in remembering that time that I realize she wasn't much older then than I am now, and yet I expected her to pick up the world, hoist it onto her shoulder and carry it around for me.

ﺰ

Step on a crack . . .

There was the dream where she fell down the stairs, backwards and in slow motion, her mouth moving but no sound escaping. I don't see myself in this dream but I must be standing at the top of the stairs watching her fall. What happened?

There was the dream where I see her body hit by a car as we are crossing the street, the fender of the car catches her and throws her up into the air, and I am standing underneath waiting for her to come down, watching her go higher and higher like a tossed ball. I wait and wait, but she just keeps going higher and higher.

There was the dream where she falls from the boat and I am sitting looking over the side she fell from, holding a life preserver in my hand and waiting for her to break the surface. Then I hear her calling to me, hear her voice saying my name again and again, pleading with me, but I will not turn to see where the voice is coming from, but keep watching the spot in the water where she went under.

. . . break your mother's back.

ii. *the apple witch*

The summer I was sixteen I tried to take my life. It's your life, my mother told me, but when it came right down to it, it wasn't really. I don't know what I was thinking, and just about the only thing I remember was that I was having the dream again.

When I was five years old I had a dream about the apple witch who lived in the dark recesses beneath the piles of apples. I was shopping with my mother, lagging behind as always, and the apple witch popped up, sending apples spilling and bruising everywhere. Her grip closed on my wrist and she pulled me screaming into the darkness after her. I remember the smell of over-ripe fruit, and the fear that no one would know where I'd gone.

❧

When I woke up in the hospital bed with my arms all taped up my mother was sitting at the side of my bed doing a book of crossword puzzles. She looked at me and said: "Pills I could have understood, Lizzie, but why would you want to damage that beautiful body of yours." At the time I thought that she didn't understand anything. I hadn't, I don't think, meant to succeed, but neither had I meant to fail if this was all the gains it reaped. But then, of course, immediately after that we went on the trip, which was all about teaching me how to live.

"I've been talking to my travel agent," my mother said. "You'd better see about getting a passport. And you'll have to let the school know you'll be gone for a while."

"A while? What kind of a while?"

"I don't know. A week, a month, a year. Hard to say really."

"Are you telling me I should drop out?"

"Well, yes, I suppose. For now. We'll just think of it as a sabbatical."

*

That was the year my mother took me to England to see the Queen and other curiosities. She wanted to take me, she said, because she was nearly forty years old and no one had ever taken her, and it didn't appear likely that anyone would now.

"I'm hardly the ingénue any more," she said. "Hardly the type any man's going to whisk away to Paris for a dirty weekend. Not that I'm saying I'd go."

My mother was going through a stage in her life where every time she passed a mirror she would stop to peer at herself quizzically, as though her reflection were a picture of someone else. A number of expressions passed through her eyes — derision, disgust, exasperation, pity, but never anything verging on approval. I didn't notice this happening at the time, or rather didn't notice myself noticing it, but later on, not so long ago, when I caught myself subjecting my reflection to the same treatment I recognized her in me, and was ashamed of myself for not telling her things at the time. Things like how beautiful she was. How proud I was. How different she was from the other mothers. I guess I never said how proud I was of her

because there were ways that she differed from the other
mothers that made me faintly ashamed and embarrassed. Like
the way she drove around with her windows rolled down
singing at the top of her voice. I was sure that people laughed
at her behind my back.

I put the trip she was planning down to the general
restlessness she was going through. I didn't give her much credit
for seeing what I was going through, although I suppose when
I cut myself up it was a pretty good hint. But even that she
treated in her queer offhand way.

*

It was when we were taking off, the moment when I
realized that the wheels of the plane were no longer touching
the runway, that I had this weird flash of being a child in my
mother's lap. I turned to her and said: "My first memory is of
flying."

"Nonsense," she said.

*

During our trip, the forced closeness imposed by spending day
and night together, sleeping in one room and often one bed,
made me feel not so much loved and protected as trapped. I
was as utterly reliant on her as a nursing infant. If, one day,
she had vanished taking the traveller's cheques and passports
with her (I lost a map our first week, and after that was entrusted
with nothing), then I would, quite likely, have simply laid down
and died. The whole trip I had nightmares about her being run
down by mad drivers in a Glasgow street, falling from a bridge
into the dirty Thames, being swept overboard during a ferry

crossing. After we went to visit the tower I even dreamt about her being beheaded. I got into the habit of touching her a lot, which she took as a sign of affection, but really I wanted to make certain that wherever she went to I would go also. If she went anywhere without me — to buy a newspaper, to pick up tickets, even to the loo in a restaurant — I resumed the childish trick of attempting to hold my breath until she returned as a charm to ward off danger. I kept a twig in my pocket so that I could touch wood at all times. I became obsessed with numbers — twos were good but threes were tricky and ones were terrifying. I tried to control our theatre seats, our train times, our room numbers to correspond with this system. I kept a travel diary, and re-reading it now I realize that I never said I, but always we.

ða

If forced to describe myself in twenty words or less I could sum myself up as a person who does not like to play games. I don't like games of sport — don't relish chasing small balls around or trying to whack things with sticks — and neither do I appreciate games of chance and the humiliation of subjecting oneself to the vagaries of fate. Games of skill were my mother's province and she treated life as one great conundrum. My mother was the only person I ever knew who carried playing cards in her purse. Calling my mother I grew accustomed to letting the rings go on, up to twenty, thirty, forty times, because if she was playing a hand of solitaire she couldn't stand to leave it until she knew how it would come out.

ða

During the time we were travelling together we made up all sorts of games to keep ourselves amused. Mom called them calisthenics for the imagination. We would make up histories for people on trains, we would decide in pubs who ought to leave with who and why, and who they would likely leave with and why. One of the games that Mom invented was Deserted Isle. It was an awful game; I hated it, and every time we played it I would end up playing out the scenarios over and over again before I could sleep at night.

What book would I take? The Bible? No, a dictionary.

What music would I want? A radio, but no the batteries would wear down. An instrument? But I couldn't play anything.

Would I choose to take a pen or a knife? I would take a knife, but my mother would take a pen.

If I could take one person with me who would it be?

iii. all fall down

The night my mother walked out on the man I thought was
my father I went blind. One minute I was sitting there in the
passenger seat of her orange Volks bug in the A&W listening
to her say: "There are things you don't know. Things I've been
meaning to tell you." The next minute everything went black.
My mother's voice went on talking, rushing at me like waves,
and that was how I knew it was only happening to me — that
it wasn't an unscheduled eclipse. Her voice sounded different
when I didn't have to look at her; disembodied, she sounded
like an overwrought actress on a radio melodrama.

&❧

I found out later that my mother used to sit by herself in the
A&W drive-in and eat order after order of onion rings. It was
what she did when she wanted to run away from home. I know
it sounds silly, she would say, but it seemed safer than hanging
around bars.

I never realized that there was a possibility she wasn't
happy.

&❧

I don't think it often happens that a person can point to a day
in her life and say on that day the door to childhood closed.
It was the longest day of the year. I remember that for some

reason. It was hot, a dead still heat that filled every corner of the house and laid us all out flat. It was so hot the air nearly had a colour. Stu was playing guitar in his bedroom and the sound was vibrating the wall between his room and mine. He kept playing the same riff over and over again. It was as constant as waves breaking and always before the next one came you knew there would be a next one. It was lulling me into a vague trance. I was sitting in my window seat, smoking a cigarette and blowing the smoke out through the screen. I was thirteen that summer, and sneaky about my smoking, even though I knew my mother would never forbid me to smoke. It wasn't the sort of thing she ever did; it wasn't within her range, so to speak. "You know what you're doing," she would say. "And if you don't, you'll learn. It's your life." It's always been my life, even when I didn't want it. When I didn't know what to do with it.

The riff that he was playing over and over began to take on words, the way that the wheels of a train will. *Walls fall down,* it said. Or else, *All fall down.* That was Stu's first electric guitar. Before that he had an acoustic that a friend of Dad's had made for him, a custom job slightly smaller than a regular guitar, made to fit Stu's childish hands. Stu was eight years old that summer, but his hands were already bigger than mine. He had the same long, tapered fingers and broad palms that Hank did. Stu was a musical prodigy. I envied him for the ease with which he picked up some new thing and made it his own, but other times I pitied him. He wasn't a child who played pick-up games of ball in the park up the street or rode skateboards up and down the sidewalks. His whole life was in his hands.

Walls fall down. I could hear my parents downstairs, my mother was saying something and Dad wasn't answering her.

I could hear her saying the same sentence over and over; it sounded like a question by the way her voice went up at the end. I couldn't make out the words she was saying, but then I wasn't trying to. It was almost suppertime; I could hear mothers up and down the street calling their children in to eat. The sounds from below were coming from the living room, though, not the kitchen, and I wondered if anybody was going to remember to make the meal. Meals in our house were a haphazard affair. When I went to my friend Miriam's house for dinner all eight family members always sat down to dinner together. No matter what else was going on they were all together at that time. To this day when I hear the word "family" I picture the McCarthys sitting round the table with their heads bowed.

❧

All fall down, said the guitar. I was looking at the tree outside my window, not thinking about anything. Rather, I was thinking but I wasn't completing thoughts, just letting them run into one another the way watercolours will on wet paper. When I was a kid Hank taught me how to mix colours and I used to spend hours at it. I'd make colours not to do anything with, not to paint pictures, not because I needed a certain colour for any particular thing, but just because I expected one day to find a new colour, one that had never been seen before. Usually I would keep mixing and re-mixing until everything had turned the colour of mud. *Walls fall down.*

There was a light tap on my half-closed door.

"Lil'bit?"

"Come in," I said.

Dad pushed the door open an inch or two further, just enough so that I could see his white, drawn face. "Family meeting," he said.

"Be right there," I said, but he was already gone. I could hear him down the hall knocking on Stu's door. The guitar stopped mid-phrase. *All. . .*

❧

I don't know where Mom thought we were going to stay the night that she walked out on Hank. We ended up spending the whole night in the hospital emergency while the doctors tried to determine why I had lost my vision. I refused to say anything to anybody. My mother kept saying, "I think she's in shock," but when the nurses asked what the possible trauma was, she didn't answer.

❧

At the family conference where our parents told us they were separating I kept waiting for Stu to cry. Everybody else was crying: my mother obliviously, the tears running down her face and into the creases of her neck; Dad, guiltily, finding himself suddenly interrupted mid-sentence by a sound halfway between a dry sob and a clearing of his throat; myself, selfishly, loudly, expressively, waiting for comfort that never came.

I can't remember the words they used, or who spoke first, although I suspect it must have been Mom. It was her decision, what she wanted. I think Hank believed that if he could allow her to go gracefully enough that there might be a chance she would come back, but I knew different. Knew, from the moment the four of us sat down around the kitchen table, that it was

all over. We would never be a family again. It was like watching
a disaster happen in slow motion, the way earthquakes are in
movies.

≈

If I had that moment in the Volks bug, sitting at the A&W, to
live over again I would be ready for it now. I would ask
questions. I would demand to know. I would find out who I
was.

≈

My sight returned, of course. Not because of anything the
doctors did or didn't do. I went to sleep that night and when
I woke up in the morning I could see again. Mom said it was
probably because I forgot I couldn't. She signed me out of the
hospital and we went to Smitty's Pancake House for breakfast
and to talk about our lives.

"What do you think we should do now, Lizzie?" Mom
asked, lighting a cigarette and absent-mindedly putting sugar
in her coffee for the third time.

I don't know if she simply forgot I was a child or if she
assumed thirteen year olds deserved absolute autonomy.

"I think I'll have waffles," I said. "With whipped cream."

"That isn't what I meant," she said. "And anyway, it won't
be cream; it'll be that crap out of a can." She took a sip of her
coffee and made a face. "God that's awful stuff."

The thing about not being able to see and then being able
to see again was that things looked different. Colours for
example. Not that they looked different exactly, but just more
themselves — sharper, harder — like the difference between

watercolours and acrylics. To this day there are shades of yellow that give me headaches.

"You know," my mother said, "if you hadn't got your vision back today they said they would have to admit you to the psych ward."

Just then the waitress came to take our order. As she was walking away Mom said, "Well, whatever job I have to take, I pray god I don't have to wear a uniform."

Later that day we checked into the YWCA. We stayed there for a week while Mom looked for an apartment. The place that she rented was a one-bedroom — all that she could afford — and I slept in a Murphy bed in the living room. At first I thought the whole thing was an adventure of kinds, but in time I grew to hate the place, its smallness and its silence. Mom was working full time and there'd be nobody there when I came home from school.

I went back to playing a game that Miriam and I used to play when we were small, a game we called *Families*. What we would do was take old magazines and catalogues and cut pictures out of them: men and women to be the parents; children and pets; houses and things to go in them. We would make up names for everybody and give them histories. Now, with Miriam across town and out of reach, I found myself playing this game again. I even found myself taking pictures from the photo album and gluing them together onto a picture of one house big enough for all of us.

ऀ

After we left Hank, my brother Stu came to us on weekends and would take over the small tidy household of women my mother and I had established. Suddenly there were empty pop bottles, discarded sneakers, and *Mad* magazines strewn everywhere. His music was almost too large for our small apartment. When he was teaching himself to play the trumpet Mom finally had to ask him not to bring it with him because the neighbours complained.

On the weekends Stu was visiting we would all make a real effort to be a family. We'd eat meals together, all sitting down at the table, and we'd go for drives in the car together or go visit Mom's folks. We tried very hard to recreate not what we'd lost but what we'd never had. By Sunday night when Hank came to pick Stu up we'd all be exhausted and Monday mornings either Mom was late for work and I was late for school or sometimes we'd both call in sick — I'd call her boss and she'd call my principal — and stay in bed all day, and end up eating granola or tinned soup for supper.

When he was about twelve Stu started making excuses about coming to visit and within a year he was hardly coming at all. It didn't seem to bother my mother any, and she just started making other plans for her weekends.

&

After the divorce, Mom started getting younger instead of older. One time, when I was in high school, I was getting dressed to go out and I went into my mother's dresser, looking for something, a necklace or something like that, and I found a small bag of grass and rolling papers in her drawer. It made me feel like I was the mother and she was the rebellious teenager. I felt absurdly old, and angry with her for not being a normal mother. I couldn't imagine anyone else's mother smoking drugs.

About a week later I checked again and the bag was gone. I never found anything like that again, and now I can see what a hypocrite I was to be so outraged, but at the time I thought it was an unforgivable lapse on her part.

≈

My mother kept the braid of my fine yellow baby hair tied up with a blue ribbon and in a plastic bag. It was in a drawer for years, and I never knew she had it until she and I unpacked our things in the new apartment. She'd gone back to the house without me to pack up. I don't know what exactly she was afraid of. That I'd get back into the house and refuse to leave, that I'd make a scene, that I'd throw a fit and end up locked away for life.

She came across the braid as she was unpacking the things that had come out of the bureau she'd shared with Hank and were going into the one she was to share with me. There was less room, less space for anything that wasn't a necessity, and that gave her the excuse to be rid of a lot of things.

"The trouble is," she told me, "that you save things so long in this life and suddenly they own you instead of the other way around."

"Throw it away if you want," I said. "It's only my old hair. It's not like I can't grow more."

"I couldn't do that, Liz," Mom said. I guess she meant not that she didn't want to. Later on, when she had the house fire, she managed to free herself from all those mementoes of the old life. I think that was why she was so manic for weeks after it happened.

❧

I didn't see much of Miriam once we moved. We were in different schools now and for a while she used to call me up and tell me about people I used to know and what they were doing, but it only made me feel more lonesome. Her parents told her she could have me stay overnight or for a weekend even, but I thought there was too much pity behind the offer. I didn't think I could face them.

❧

After my mother and I first left, I didn't want to go back to the house, didn't want to see Hank until I had worked out what my relation to him was. I was angrier with my mother than with him; her lie was larger, more self-serving. My rage with her was boundless; it needed something the size of a mountain to contain it, but it was a rage with nowhere to go. I could not afford to be angry with her because if she was gone I would have nothing. My mother was still my mother, for better or worse, but Hank was more difficult to define.

One time, I'd gone to spend a weekend with Hank and Stu when Mom was off somewhere. I slept in my old room. Except that it wasn't my old room any more. It was the same room: same wallpaper with the pink cabbage roses that hid demon faces; same hardwood floors with the scratch marks from all the times I'd moved my furniture around, and in the door frame my initials where I'd carved them in with my scout knife. But it was Hank's storage room now, and there were rolled-up canvases piled up against one wall and his framing tools all over the place. It was obvious I didn't belong there.

It was obvious too how the separation had divided us into a house of men and a house of women. Hank hated to cook and we had spaghetti two nights and went out for burgers on the third. The whole house had a stripped-down look, like a ship's cabin where there was no unnecessary article. I avoided Hank as much as I could, because I was afraid that none of the old rules applied and I didn't know the new ones.

I'm not even sure whose idea it was that I go and stay there — if it was an attempt on someone's part to heal the rift between Hank and me. That was the last time I went back to the house. I told my mother when she came back that she couldn't make me go there. "It's up to you," she said. "It's your life."

iv. beginnings, middles and endings

My mother is a writer. In speaking of my mother I find it almost
impossible to employ the past tense. She was not always a
writer. She says that first she was a daughter, then a wife, then
a mother; then she decided it was time to make time for herself.

The summer I was ten she started taking classes at the
Saskatchewan School of the Arts. The school was located near
Fort Qu'Appelle in an old tuberculosis sanatorium. All four of
us drove down there. My mother was nervous, jumpy. She
asked Dad over and over if he was sure he knew where he
was going. She kept taking her sunglasses off and cleaning
them with her white cotton skirt. Dad was singing a song that
he'd made up, a sloppy sort of blues song that would accom-
modate any occasion. "My woman done left me," he sang. "My
woman done gone to summer camp. Don't know what I done
wrong, but my woman say she movin' on."

"Oh cut it out, Hank," my mother said, but she was
laughing.

Stu picked up the song. "My mama done left me," he
piped. "I'll be eating peanut butter sandwiches all day long."

Dad called the school a summer camp for adults, but when
we got there we found that most of the adults were there
dropping off their children for the band programs, the dance
classes and drama classes. It didn't seem right to be dropping
off our mother. There were kids running wild all over the place,
a bunch playing volleyball on the lawn out front, some in

bathing suits filing on to an old yellow school bus, older ones lounging on the steps. There were a bunch of kids wearing kilts and T-shirts, there for the piping class.

Mom registered in the main building, the big brick one with wings shooting off to either side. Stu and I sat on the step out front to wait while she and Dad went in. A girl my age with lopsided, greenish-blonde braids came and sat down on the step beside us.

"I play the clarinet," she said. "I've been here for a week already. What are you here for?" She put the tail of one of her braids in her mouth and sucked on it.

"We're dropping off our mother," I said. "She's a writer."

"Oh," said the girl. Then she stood up and went running down the wooden sidewalk to catch up with two other girls.

Dad and Mom came back out of the building, Mom holding a piece of paper and a key.

"A room of my own," she said. "Just think of it." Dad made a face, but she didn't see him.

ta.

One time, when Mom was staying with me, I overheard her on the phone talking to somebody about the year she was pregnant. I was about to walk into the room and ask her something but instead I remained on the wrong side of the door, listening.

"Even though I was getting bigger all the time it felt like I was disappearing, do you know what I mean? I'd look in the mirror and there'd be nobody there — just this huge pink smock and these pigtails like a child would wear. It began to frighten me — I had to stop wearing make-up because I couldn't see my face in the mirror to put it on. When Hank asked me, I told

him I'd developed an allergy. It wasn't like that when I was
carrying Elizabeth — but then of course I felt like Hester Prynne.
And then, after he was born, it went away and I was back in
the mirror when I looked. I might not have always liked what
I saw, but at least I was there."

&

Mom's room was in a small building back of the main building.
When we walked in we were in a room that was a cross between
a living room and a dentist's outer office. There was a group
of people sitting around there talking to each other, and a
bearded fellow off to the side reading a book. A tall man stood
up from the group and shook Mom's hand. He asked her who
she was and welcomed her to Fort San. The other people
introduced themselves and Mom shook hands with all of them.
Then she said, "Oh, these are my children," with a small wave
of her hand that made me feel we shouldn't have been there
at all. Then Dad came through the door, weighed down with
Mom's suitcase.

"Room 12?" Mom asked. "Can anybody tell me where it is?"

"Top of the stairs next to the showers," said the man who'd
been reading a book.

As we were going up the stairs Dad whispered to my
mother, "Communal showers? Co-ed dorms?"

"Oh grow up," my mother said.

My mother's room was small and plain. There was a bed
and a desk and chair and that was all. I couldn't see that it was
anything to be excited about but she kept turning around and
around and beaming at all of it. She put her suitcase into the

little closet and her carry-all on the desk. Then she sat down on the bed and looked at the three of us standing there.

"I guess you guys will be wanting to hit the road," she said. "If you're going to make it to Regina for supper and all."

"I thought . . . " said Dad and then stopped. I knew what he thought, that we were going to look around together, maybe drive into Fort Qu'Appelle for supper. Get Mom settled, is how we'd phrased it when we were making plans. Now it was pretty obvious that Mom didn't need us here. She'd found what she wanted.

"You kids run down to the car," Dad said. "I'll be right there."

When we got out into the hall I saw that there was a door at the end that opened onto a fire escape. We went out the door and sat on the steps. We could hear a disjointed version of the theme from the *Muppet Show* being played in the building next to the parking lot. I couldn't quite make out what the song was until Stu started to hum it.

"I wish I was coming here," said Stu.

"I don't," I said. "I hate it."

❧

My mother wrote stories that had beginnings, middles and endings. They were, I think, good stories, although for years I was unable to read them. She only published two books in her lifetime, and according to the critics, her greatest book was the one she didn't live to write. I come across her name in studies of Canadian literature these days and the word most often used in connection with her name is "promise". They say that it is unfortunate that she didn't live to fulfil her promise. Of course they know nothing about her.

ॐ

My mother did all her writing longhand. For years I believed that she couldn't type, and might never have found out otherwise if she hadn't been reduced to secretarial positions to support the two of us.

"But, you can't type," I said to her.

"Oh, no," she said. "I just can't type and think at the same time."

ॐ

In the years of my middle adolescence, Mom went through a brief period of fame. She was a well-known Prairie author, an up and coming Canadian author. She was on her way. She gave readings at universities and bookstores from Saskatoon all the way out to the West Coast and the Island. She went on Morningside and talked about how difficult it was to be a wife and mother and still have time to write. She talked about Virginia Woolf and a recent study that showed that most of the best-known women writers had been childless. I hated her. I refused to read her book. I accidentally heard her reading on a local radio program. The story had a narrator with a teenage daughter who cut her hair with manicure scissors and refused to go to school. I went to the library and took the book off the shelf and into the bathroom where I shredded the pages and flushed them down the toilet. In the two local bookstores that carried it I took less drastic measures and merely buried it beneath stacks of books about Saskatoon street names or biographies of Lester B. Pearson.

ᢞ

My mother's handwriting always looked like she was writing in a moving vehicle. When we were living in the apartment together I used to find scraps of paper with story ideas and notes all over the house. She'd scribble on the margins of my homework, write on the envelopes of letters addressed to me, rip pages out of magazines.

"Stop writing on everything," I said to her, waving an envelope under her nose.

"Stop writing?" she said, like I'd asked her to stop breathing.

"Can't you respect me at all? My things?"

"Oh, I see, Liz," she took off her glasses to look at me. "You're still mad that I put you in a story. You should be flattered, really. Not everybody has a mother who is a published writer."

She didn't understand, maybe never understood, where she ended and I began. It was all the same to her. It was all material.

v. the hoodoos and other mysteries

Our big trip out west was one of the last things we ever did as a family.

The summer I was nine years old we were to take a family vacation and drive to the mountains, maybe even all the way through to the coast. I think the marriage was beginning to come unravelled by then. My mother was taking a few classes at the university that year, and working part time in the Arts & Sciences library. She had friends of her own again, interests that were outside the marriage. She'd begun to contradict Dad in public, instead of just listening to him talk, and smiling and nodding. She'd had her hair cut short and streaked and had a new nervous habit of ruffling it all up with her hand and then smoothing it down like someone playing with the fur on the scruff of a dog's neck.

We had one of those pop-up tent trailers that we'd borrowed from another family who lived on the block. I think it was the loan of the trailer that decided my parents on taking this trip instead of just driving up to the cabin like we usually did. There was a sense of event, of expectation, in the days leading up to the trip. Dad bought a Coleman stove, my mother planned and re-planned what clothes and food we should take. There were lists all over the house, written on the covers of magazines, on the backs of envelopes, even minuscule lists on matchbook covers. I took my cat Cleopatra over to stay with my friend Miriam. Stu was allowed one shoebox full of toys for the trip and he spent days taking things out of it and putting them back in. My mother had bought me a number of new Nancy Drew mysteries for the trip, but wouldn't tell me how many. They were hidden away so that I wouldn't try to read them before we were actually on our way.

At first the drive promised to be a good one. My mother was relaxed, smiling at Dad even when he wasn't looking. Dad was singing, "You are My Sunshine", a song from the hammock days when the sky was close and familiar. Stu was happy, in his fat, solid Stu way. He was driving his matchbox cars up and down the grooves in the upholstery, over my legs, into the ashtray, up and down the armrest. He was humming, never the same song as Dad, but usually the one he'd just finished singing. It didn't seem to bother him or distract him that Dad was making a noise completely different from his noise. He never hummed loudly enough that he could be heard in the front seat. My mother would be reading a map, not because she needed to know where we were going but just because she loved maps.

"Hank," she said. "Use these three words in a sentence: Climax, Elbow, Plenty."

"Maybe later," he said.

"Bienfait," she said. "There's a town named Bienfait, do you know what that means?" That was for me, because I was taking French lessons.

"They pronounce it *Bean-fate*," said Hank.

"No, not really," said Mom, appalled and delighted.

"Really," said Hank.

She would read off the names of small Saskatchewan and Alberta towns and speculate on the lives of the people who lived there. "Livelong," she'd say. "Do you think they really do?"

ð

The first night we spent in the trailer I learned that Stu hummed
even in his sleep. Our parents were in the bunk on one side
of the trailer and Stu and I on the other. Stu didn't exactly snore,
he just exhaled each breath on a different note. Dad snored so
loud the walls of the tent shook. My mother didn't sleep at all.
I woke once in the middle of the night and saw her reading
by the light of a fresh candle and smoking. I couldn't make out
what book she was reading, and I didn't want to move my
head too much or she would know I was awake. The candlelight
made the hollows in her cheeks and under her eyes look more
prominent, and she frightened me a little. She was smoking,
sitting up with the sleeping bag pushed down to her waist. She
was wearing an old Black Watch flannel shirt of Dad's, unbut-
toned and pulled loosely closed. Her hair looked like a little
boy's, like Stu's, when it wasn't all combed into a style. She
looked completely alone, as if she was in a room where she
went often to smoke and to read without any hands pulling at
her or voices battling for attention. I think it was that, her
apartness, that made me afraid to move, nervous of alerting her
that I was watching.

In the morning the candle had been reduced to a puddle
of wax and the ashtray was full of the smoked-down butts of
her menthol cigarettes. I think that was the first time I was ever
conscious of my mother having a life of her own, a life that
didn't include any of us. In the car that day, back on the road,
I kept watching her for signs that this wasn't her life — that
her true life was the one when the rest of the world was sleeping
and there was no one to answer to. Once, when she was looking

out the window, I saw something of that peaceful expression on her face and I pinched Stu's leg so that he let out an involuntary wail. She turned back to us then, her forehead creased with annoyance. "It was an accident," I said.

≈

The expression on her face — it was like she was aloft in a hot air balloon and we were all rapidly diminishing to the size and importance of ants on the ground below. It was as though soon we would grow too small to be seen, disappear, never have existed at all. This, at least, is what I imagine later, years later, trying to remember why I had grown suddenly enraged at the sight of my mother, reading a book and smoking a cigarette.

≈

We stopped in Drumheller to see the dinosaur museum. While we were all looking at something else, Stu crawled under a rope to see one of the skeletons up close. None of us saw this part, although Stu said later that was what he had done. The first thing we saw was a man in a uniform holding Stu by his collar like he was a disobedient puppy to be grabbed by the scruff of the neck.

"Is this your boy?" he asked my mother.

The funny thing about all this was the way that Stu looked while the guard was holding him. Stu wasn't there. It was Stu's shell that the guard had hold of, but Stu himself had managed to elude his grasp by leaving his body behind. I asked him later where he'd gone but he couldn't tell me.

ع

One summer when Stu was small, about six maybe, the year we bought the deep freeze anyway, he started saving the bones from dinner every time we had beef for supper. He saved T-bones, ribs, whatever. He'd clean off the meat as best he could and then put them in a box under his bed. This went on for weeks and nobody knew he was doing it until Mom looked under his bed one day. She was looking for something but she wouldn't say what and anyway it didn't matter once she found this weird box of bones. When Stu got home she called him into the kitchen where she had the box sitting on the table.

"What does this mean, Stuie?" she asked. "What are you doing with these bones?"

He was building a cow puzzle.

ع

The first thing that happened on that trip, the first sign, as it were, was the hail. This was in the middle of the afternoon, right after we'd stopped for lunch. We'd all had pie and ice cream. "We're on vacation," my mother told the waitress. The hailstones were the size of crab apples at first; they made a wonderful noise as they struck the roof. I was trying to figure out what the sound behind the sound of the hail was when I realized it was Stu's silence. Then my mother began to laugh, wildly and gleefully, like a child watching the schoolhouse burn to the ground.

"It's not funny," Dad said.

"But it is," my mother said.

The hailstones were the size of Christmas oranges or babies' fists now, and we could see the pings and dints they were leaving on the trunk of the car. Dad pulled the car over to the shoulder.

"Stop it," he said to my mother. "Just cut it out."

She was still laughing when the hailstone hit the windshield on her side making a small beautiful spider web. Then she stopped. "You're right," she said. "It's not funny at all."

We sat there quietly until the hail stopped and then Dad got out, slammed the door and walked around the car three times. He didn't seem to be looking for damage, more like he was trying to cast a spell. Then he got in the car, started it up again, and pulled back into traffic.

ຈະ

I can't remember if it was before or after Drumheller that we stopped to see the Hoodoos. When my mother took me to England one of the things we saw was a Henry Moore exhibit at the Tate Gallery for which I felt an immediate affinity, like an acquaintance from a past life. The Hoodoos were better, though, because they weren't intentional. Nor were they inviolable. Stu and I spent the afternoon climbing in and out of them, through narrow passages that sometimes went at right angles through the stone so you could enter into darkness and then turn out into the light. I've never been back there and it's one of those places almost impossible to believe you haven't invented.

ຈະ

After Drumheller, but before the mountains, we were to stop in Calgary to visit an uncle of Hank's, his father's older brother. This uncle had paid for Hank's tuition when he was at University. Hank's parents had died when he was fifteen and he had been shuffled around from relative to relative. The uncle and his wife had moved to Calgary years before and Dad hadn't seen them since his graduation. We got lost and finally my mother made Dad stop at a pay phone and call them to tell us how to get there. When we pulled onto their street there was an old man standing in the driveway, waving. Dad parked the car on the street because the trailer wouldn't fit in the driveway.

Dad got out of the car without shutting off the ignition, and the rest of us stayed in the car and waited. The old man said something to Dad, and then came over and looked into the back seat of the car. Stu was asleep, curled into a snail shape on the seat beside me. I knew that I should smile at the old guy, that was the polite thing to do, but there was something in his eyes that frightened me. He half turned and spoke to Dad. "So this is the . . . " and then he barked. I suppose it was a laugh but it sounded like a bark, or like something being pulled loose. Something old and rotten and dead at the roots.

Whatever it was he said made Dad's face close up. He shook his head, like a boxer reeling from a punch and then walked past the old man and got in the car. He drove down the street, back past the gas station where we'd stopped to use the phone, and kept on going out of the city. I started to say something once, but my mother's hand came back between the seats and touched mine in a way that said, "Not now." I never did learn what the old man said. Dad would never talk about it, or him, or that visit again. Knowing what I do now, I can guess, but what I haven't worked through yet is why Hank reacted as he did. Where that barb lodged itself in him.

≈

We never made it to the mountains; after Calgary we turned back the way we'd come. Maybe if we hadn't stopped in Calgary, if we'd gone straight through to the Rockies, then things would have turned out differently.

≈

Stu claims that he doesn't remember anything of that trip. "But it's in the song you played at the funeral," I said. I can hear it in the song. He says that's because when he plays that song he isn't really playing, that there's no composition to it, that he is receiving. At her funeral I was thinking of us in the car, dreaming of something large and solid like a eighteen-wheel rig that would overtake us, take us all at once in a fearful collision. All of us together.

vi. family time

The happiest years of my life were the ones I can barely remember.

When I was five years old we moved to Saskatoon; Dad cut off his pony tail and went to work teaching high school. My mother was pregnant with Stu that year. She referred to that year, 1973, as the year we became domestic animals. Up until then we'd been living in a semi-winterized log cabin at Emma Lake, heated mainly by a woodstove in the kitchen. During the year Dad drove a school bus in Prince Albert and in the summers none of us did anything. My memories from that time are all misty around the edges. It doesn't seem like a real part of my life at all. I remember the taste of fresh-picked chokecherries on warm days; standing in the lake and letting the minnows kiss against my legs; making beds out of pine boughs in the yard and lying there safe in the darkness while my father taught me the sky. I don't remember any of the constellations now except for the names — a song with which to lull myself to sleep. The three of us used to lie in the hammock strung between the two big trees back of the house and the woodshed. I would be in the middle with the large safe bodies of my mother and father on either side of me. We would lie there for hours, my parents drinking their homemade wine, the hammock rocking steadily back and forth, my father singing in his warm, raspy voice.

❧

For the longest time I thought my first day of school was the
worst day of my life. We'd moved to the city three weeks before
and were living in a tiny apartment that we stayed in until just
after Christmas of that year. The school was just up the street
from us, a great brick castle or prison from an old fairy tale.
Mom was supposed to walk me to school. She promised Dad
before he left for work that she would take me, but by the time
I was ready to go she was locked in the bathroom making this
terrible noise. She was either crying or being sick. I knocked
and knocked on the door but she didn't answer.

The school was huge and named for a dead King. It isn't
there anymore.

I humiliated myself the first day of school. I wasn't the
child who wet her pants because I was scared to put up my
hand and ask to leave. It was a little blonde wisp of a thing
named Lorie, or maybe Lallie, who peed down her leg into a
puddle beneath her desk, and then wept with silent shame. I
wasn't that child.

When the teacher asked me what my name was I said I
didn't know. Dad called me Bit or Lil'bit, and Mom called me
Liz or Lizzie. It wasn't that I didn't know my name, just that I
didn't know who I was supposed to be at school.

"What's your name?"

"I don't know."

She went to her desk and looked at her list of names, like
she was going to pick one out and give it to me.

"You won't get very far here if you don't know who you
are. Won't you tell me your name?"

By this time I had been struck utterly mute.

The other children laughed. Even little Lallie or Lorie with the puddle underneath her desk laughed.

"Your name is Elizabeth Young."

Nobody ever called me Elizabeth.

≈

I had an idea that we'd come to the city because the baby was coming. That if not for the baby our life could've gone on as it was forever. I didn't really think about me having to start school or any of that. It was obvious that the baby was the important thing.

≈

Dad did a painting for me, of me, when we moved from the lake to the city. He laid out a large piece of heavy white paper on the living room floor and got me to lie down on it, and then he took a black felt marker and traced my outline. Then he got out his paints and asked me to tell him all the things I was going to miss about living at the lake.

"The beach," I said, and he filled the feet in the colour of sand.

"The lake," I said, and he painted clear blue water up to the waist.

"The minnows," I said, and he painted in minnows up to the knees.

"The trees," I said, and he painted evergreen branches from the wrists to the shoulders.

"The sunset," I said, and he painted a pinky-red semi-circle on the belly and then a line and another semi-circle beneath it. "The caw birds," I said, and he painted three crows on the chest in the sky above the sun.

"Wild strawberries," I said, and he filled in the hands with minute and perfect strawberries.

"The sky at night," I said, and he filled my head with stars.

%

My mother changed when we moved into the city. Everything was different that year but my mother most of all. She became, for the first time, a wife. She and Dad were married that year, but that isn't what I mean exactly, and anyway I didn't find out about that until later. I mean that she began to cook meals for the family, to vacuum under things instead of around them, to dress like one of the smiling ladies from the Eaton's catalogue. She had new, brightly-coloured clothes. Most of our old clothes, the ones we bought at the Thrift Shop, went in the garbage. She got fussier about the way I looked too, and stopped letting me wear whatever I wanted all the time. She read recipe books and baked cakes even when it wasn't anybody's birthday.

%

Miriam McCarthy was my very best friend in the world from the day I met her. I would go over to her house in my blue dress and come home in her green one. It used to drive our mothers crazy. One year for Christmas my mother made Miriam and I matching red flannel nightgowns with white eyelet lace around the necks, and even these we would trade back and forth. As we got older my hair darkened while Miriam's stayed that pale baby blonde, and then my eyes changed from blue to green. By fourth grade she was several inches taller than I

was and the shape of our faces had both changed to the point
where the resemblance was lost.

I was in awe of Miriam's whole family: her father who
pretended he couldn't tell us apart, "Which one of you's mine?"
he'd ask in a voice of mock dismay; her mother who was always
in the kitchen, making supper or baking cookies; her sisters
Colleen and Heather who seemed so grown up and glamorous
with their page boy haircuts and their rooms that smelled of
sweet perfume; her brothers Neil and Murray, who were always
teasing us; her granny who was always sitting in the living
room, and knitting or dozing in front of the television.

We'd sit down to dinner and Mr. McCarthy would bow
his head and everyone would go silent instantly and close their
eyes. He never prayed aloud, just moved his lips for a moment
and then said *Amen*, and then everybody said *Amen* and
everything started up again exactly where it left off. I was the
only one who ever opened their eyes during the prayer. I tried
not to, every time I promised myself I wouldn't, but I couldn't
help sneaking a look at them all silently moving their lips, trying
to make out what they were saying.

ॐ

When we came to the city, our world expanded to make room
for other people. Mom and Dad would have other couples over
in the evenings, people that Dad knew from the school he was
teaching at or old friends from college. They would play bridge
or just sit around and listen to records. I would fall asleep at
night to unfamiliar voices and the strained sound of my mother's
laughter.

❧

Miriam liked my house too, for reasons I couldn't understand. Mom's domesticity came and went. Some days we'd be lucky to get fed at all, sometimes there'd be chili in a big pot on the stove, or stuff for sandwiches in the fridge. Mom would often forget about it altogether and then she'd order out for Chinese or run down and pick up a bucket of chicken. We usually ate in the living room so that we could watch TV. There was a dining room table but Mom had gradually overtaken the dining room and turned it into an office, so if you wanted to eat in there you had to pick up all the papers and move the typewriter. Our first year in the city we ate Christmas dinner off of TV tables and in the middle of it I started to cry. I couldn't help thinking about all the McCarthy's sitting down to the big table and then that moment when they all bowed their heads together.

❧

There was a thunderstorm the day Stu was born.

Dad came into my room in the middle of the night and bundled me up in the quilt I was sleeping under and I didn't waken until we were in the car, stopped in front of the McCarthys' house.

"It's time, Bit," he said. "The baby's coming." He lifted me out of the back seat and carried me around to the front of the car and opened the door so I could kiss my mother. She kissed me back and put her hand on my hair but she didn't seem to be looking at me.

"Go to Miriam's after school," Dad said. "We'll call you."

Then he got back into the car and he and my mother drove away, and I remember feeling like they were going off on some great adventure without me.

Mrs. McCarthy was standing on the front steps in her nightgown and robe and she took me from his arms. She carried me into the house and put me into the bed where Miriam was sleeping. When I woke up in the morning Miriam was already up and getting ready for school. I had to wear one of her dresses because Dad had forgotten the bag I had packed for when the baby came.

It was during the quiet time at school that morning, the time when we were supposed to put our heads down on our desks and rest, that I saw the sky outside the window open up and the rains pour down. At recess when we were told to stay in the mudrooms to play, I put on my coat and went outside and sat on the steps to the playground alone watching the skies break open and the sudden light. I knew where babies came from, knew that the new life was already in my mother's stomach waiting to be born. And still I thought that he would come from the sky.

ã

I don't think I've ever loved anyone as much as I loved my brother when they brought him home from the hospital. For the first year of his life we shared a bedroom, and every night before I went to sleep I would talk to him. He would lie sleeping in his crib and I would tell him things: how to mix colours to get other colours, the names of stars, the words I had learned to spell, stories, songs, how to build a snowman, anything that occurred to me. I tried to tell him about who we were, what we'd been doing before he came along. I told him what I knew about where he came from and about the day I saw the sky open. I never prayed when I was a child, but somehow, telling my baby brother all I knew about life so far, I came close.

☙

Stu looked like Dad with my mother's green eyes, but I didn't look like anybody. I used to go through Mom's family albums trying to find my features represented in some other face. Even before my mother told me the truth about myself I'd begun to suspect I was adopted. I was wrong of course. I was my mother's daughter.

vii. the memory song

In the days and weeks after the funeral I played solitaire and found that the click of the cards against my mother's old oak table comforted me. I gave away most of her clothes and kept some. I went to a bookstore on Broadway and asked them to put a display of her books in the window. I resolved to be proud of her. I emptied her small rented house of all her possessions and found that there was room enough for her most important things among mine. I remembered her saying, *they're only things*, after the fire. I quit going to classes for awhile, called some of my professors and told them what had happened. Then it got close to exam time and it seemed easier to go in and write them than to have them deferred and so I went back. I brought Mom's cat home and changed its name to Alice so that from now on, I would always be Spike.

❧

"If you really want to know the truth about yourself," said Stu, "why don't you ask your father?"

"But I don't know who he is," I said. "I don't know how to find him. I don't even know if he wants to be found."

"I don't mean him. He doesn't matter. I mean Hank, he's your real father. I always thought you had more smarts than this. Maybe I gave you too much credit."

❧

Hank is the sort of man who looks like he shot up a foot in height one night when he was sixteen and never grew accustomed to his size. The only time he loses his gawkiness is when he is painting. With a brush in his hand he manages to escape his body, to turn it into something that moves colour across a canvas. For a while he dabbled with photography but he broke too many lenses and could never hold his camera steady enough. Stu grew to almost the same height as Hank, but turned out thinner, not skinny but lean. Stu's way of inhabiting his body is different from Hank's and his collisions with the real world are less frequent. Once after I'd been to visit Hank, my mother asked: "Does he still rub his eyes with balled-up fists when he's tired?" It was a gesture that made him look like a little boy, made you want to throw him over your shoulder like a sack of potatoes and carry him off to dreamland. It was a ridiculous and pathetic gesture. The fact that she remembered it, asked about it, made me realize that she had loved him once.

ِ

Hank remarried a few years after the divorce, a woman named Joyce who I could never convince myself to like.

I don't think he ever got over my mother though. Stu said the most interesting thing about Joyce was how ordinary she was. "You wouldn't think a person could really be that ordinary, that boring," he said. "At first I thought it had to be a cover for something but it's not. There's absolutely nothing going on under the surface."

ِ

I went to see an exhibit of Hank's paintings one time. Stu talked
me into going to the opening with him. I'd planned to slip in
one day, mid-afternoon, and look around without having to
actually talk to anybody about it. I still wasn't really easy with
Hank; the years right after the separation had marked out a
distance between us.

Hank's wife, Joyce, was with him and I kept watching the
two of them together. When people are couples you can usually
get the sense of them together by the way they stand, the way
each one knows exactly how their body fits into the other's. It
wasn't that Hank and Joyce didn't make sense together, because
they did in a way. He was tall and she was small and soft and
round, with dimples in her cheeks and on the backs of her
hands. When she stood beside him her head was at about the
level of his third rib, and every so often he would suddenly
become aware of her there and raise his arm so that she could
be tucked under his wing. When I was looking at the two of
them together I was trying to remember if Hank and my mother
had ever fit each other so comfortably. Any photographs of
them would have gone in the fire, but there were no pictures
in my memory of the two of them together. It was like they'd
never happened.

&

It wasn't until I began consciously trying to remember that I
realized how much I'd forgotten.

My other first memory is of being in the canoe with Dad,
lying in the bottom of it between the stern and the middle seat.

This memory is made up entirely of sound. I can hear the
waves making a slapping noise against the sides of the boat,

the rhythm of the water dividing in front of the boat and closing after it. This is a reconstructed memory — I remember the sound and must imagine the rest like a blind person at the movies. But it is a verifiable memory, it really happened. Mom told me that Hank used to take me out in the canoe all the time, even when I was really small. She said that when I was a baby if I was fussing about anything the only thing that would calm me down was being out on the water.

❧

Hank still owned the house where we had lived as a family. The house was on a street that was easy for me to avoid so I was not particularly conscious of avoiding it, didn't realize I had been until I pulled up in front of the house and saw that it was a different colour from what I remembered. I didn't talk to Hank before I went to see him. Stu arranged the meeting for me. He said he would make sure that Joyce wouldn't be around so that I could talk to Hank alone. "But you'll be there," I said. "No," he said. "I don't think so. Better you two are on your own."

I sat in the car for a few minutes staring at the house. The sun was shining; it was one of those soft late-summer days. The trees in front of the house were taller than I'd expected. A spruce that had been the same height as me the year we moved into the house was now up to the windows of the second story.

I hadn't spoken to Hank at the funeral. The family were seated separately, in a little room to the side of the chapel, and after the service he disappeared. I hadn't seen him again, between the time of the funeral and showing up at his front door.

When Hank answered the door I couldn't think what to say to him — all the words I'd rehearsed in the car on the way over rang false.

"You painted the house blue," I said, inanely.

"Yes," he said. "A few years back. Come in."

He held the door open for me and then we were both standing in the alcove, almost touching but not quite and I couldn't think what was the appropriate gesture to make. How do you greet a man who used to be your father? I thought perhaps I should hug him but instead I dropped my purse and he moved back to let me pick it up and then the moment had passed and we walked into the living room.

"This is nice," I said, waving my hand vaguely at the room. It wasn't though, it was awful.

"Well, it's Joyce mostly," Hank said. "You know me, I don't pay much attention to that stuff."

You know me, he said. But I didn't, not really.

"Maybe we could sit in the kitchen," he said. "There's tea. I don't know, do you drink tea?"

"Yes," I said. "Fine. Tea is fine."

The kitchen was better, more itself. There was the same old square wooden table and chairs and everything was still the right colour. I relaxed a little, sat down on a chair, told myself it was going to be all right.

"I'm sorry," said Hank.

"Sorry?" I said.

"About Bea."

"Oh," I said. "Right, of course." At the funeral, in the reception line after, I kept seeing the whole thing as theatre of the absurd. Every time somebody came up and took me by the hand and said, "I'm sorry." I would think, Oh, was it your fault? Sorry, sorry, I'm so sorry, we're all so sorry.

"How do you think Stu's doing?" asked Hank. "I'm a little worried, myself."

Stu had announced just after the funeral that he wasn't going to go back to school in the fall. He said he'd only been waiting to turn sixteen anyway. He thought he might go travelling.

"I've told him that he's welcome to stay here as long as he wants," said Hank. "I mean, that goes without saying. It's his home."

Yes, I thought, *his* home.

"Stu will be okay," I said. "That is, I'm sure he will. He's got his own ways of coping with things." Actually, I hadn't been thinking much of Stu at all, of his grief. I was too busy with my own.

Hank set the teapot and cups down on the table, put some cookies from a glass jar onto a plate and set it down beside the teapot. I looked at the cookies; they were oatmeal, home-baked.

"Those look good," I said, but I didn't take one.

Hank poured tea into one of the cups, frowned at it and took the lid off the teapot to pour it back in.

"How's your work going?" I asked.

"You don't have to make small talk with me, Lil'bit," he said.

"No, I know," I said. "I mean, I'm not."

"That isn't why you're here," he said.

"No, it's not."

He poured out the tea and pushed my cup over to me. I took hold of it, glad to have something to hold onto. He forgot to offer me milk and sugar and I didn't ask. I didn't ask because I realized that maybe he was nervous too.

"You called me Lil'bit," I said. "Nobody's called me that in years. I'd almost forgotten."

"Does it bother you? I can call you something else if you'd rather. I know Stu calls you Best, but I still think of you as Lil'bit."

"No," I said. "It's okay. I kind of like it actually." I smiled.

"You look like her," he said.

"You think so, really? I've never been able to see it. I mean my hair's a different colour, our eyes are, were, different colours."

"It's the character that shapes the face. She's very strong in you."

"Good," I said. "I'm glad."

"Stu told me you have questions, and I'll answer them all as best I can, but will you do something for me first?"

"What?" I asked. "I mean, yes, of course."

"Tell me how it is with you," he said. "Tell me about your life."

≈

I used to love watching Hank paint. When we moved into the house he had a real studio for the first time and he used the extra space as incentive to let his canvases grow larger and larger. When he painted he used his whole body; he went at the canvas with brushes, palette knives, and sticks. After a few hours work he would be drenched in sweat, his shirt sticking to him and his hair wildly standing up and matted with paint where he had pushed it back from his eyes.

When I remember how he painted it strikes me that it was the only time he ever seemed to inhabit his body completely — where there didn't seem to be some delay between the signal sent from the brain and the corresponding reaction in one of his limbs.

We played a game where I would watch him mix his paints and make up names for the new colours. We played other games too, like he would show me a finished canvas and make me try to guess which way was up. Sometimes when he was starting a fresh work he would let me put the first stroke of paint on the canvas and he would use it as his starting point. Usually by the time he finished my little dab of paint would have vanished under the layers he had added, but I always knew it was there.

&

Hank had loved my mother from the first moment he saw her.

"She was the most beautiful woman I ever knew. I was awed by her. Unfortunately she knew it."

I don't remember this.

"But she was wild, different, she didn't fit."

My mother told me once that she was thrown out of — asked to leave — a Saskatoon tavern because she was wearing slacks in a time when they were not considered acceptable attire. Was this what wild was? She also told me that in high school the not-nice girls were the ones who sat on boys' laps and rode in their cars.

"After grade twelve ended she took off. Disappeared."

"Where did she go?"

"I'm not sure really. A lot of places. She never wrote me the whole time she was gone — nearly two years — but she'd send your grandparents postcards every few weeks. They never said much, mainly just that she was still alive and not to worry. And not to try and find her. Your grandfather used to bring me the cards a couple of days after they received them. He'd let me keep them. Said he didn't want them around the house anyway. He used to look at me like he despised me, like I was a maimed animal that deserved to be shot. Because I wasn't man enough to make your mother marry me and settle down. To turn her into what everybody thought she should be. Of course that was the last thing I ever wanted her to be, at least that's what I thought then, and now I think I was probably right."

"So why did she ever come home then. Why didn't she keep on running."

"You. You brought her home, and back to me. Only she wasn't the same any more."

What happened was that my mother phoned Hank from Vancouver to tell him that she was pregnant and that she didn't know what to do. He flew out there and spent a week with her and then brought her home. Bea called her parents and said that she and Hank were married and on their way home. Shortly after they got back to Saskatoon they announced I was on the way. Everybody knew that lies were being told, but it seemed best not to ask too many direct questions. I was, of course, slightly premature, but a healthy weight despite that.

"I always thought that we would tell you eventually. Once I thought I was going to lose you both when your mother persuaded me that she wanted to go to the west coast and show you to your father."

"What happened?"

"You came back. You both came back and I never asked."

"I suppose he didn't want me."

The pressure building inside my head. The sound of bells. My mother holding me so tight it felt like a punishment.

"That was the second time she left me and the second time she came back. And then after that we had Stu and I thought that would hold us together."

"Why did you let her leave the third time?"

"Because there was never anything I could do to stop her."

"Why was she so selfish? Did she ever think of us?"

"You shouldn't say things like that."

"But they're true, aren't they?"

"Does it really matter any more? She's gone."

It matters.

ঽ

As a small form of exquisite torture, I go into the cosmetics section of department stores to try on perfume — *l'air du temps*, the scent my mother wore. When I was a child the smell of that perfume meant that my mother was going somewhere special, that her blonde hair would all be pulled back into a French twist and she would be wearing something dark and soft that swished as she walked. When she kissed me goodnight before leaving the house her perfume would leave a ghost of itself on my pillow to console me until her return.

≥

Stu came in then. He didn't look like a kid anymore. He hugged Hank first and then came over to me and just took both my hands in his.

"Okay?" he asked. Or maybe it wasn't a question at all.

≥

The first birthday party I had in the city, Hank made me a piñata, but when it came time for all the children to gather round and strike at it with sticks I threw a blue fit, as my mother always called it, and finally my mother went to the store and bought candy to replace the treats that were hidden inside the magical fish with scales of every colour imaginable. For years, up until Mom and I moved out, it hung in my room over my bed and before I went to sleep I would reach up and tap its tail so that it twirled in circles above me until all the colours ran together and I fell asleep.

≥

I thought that all the photos of us as a family were lost in the fire, but it never occurred to me that Hank might have had any pictures, that he would have kept them.

Hank set up the slide projector and got out the boxes of slides and then left Stu and me alone to watch them.

"You can stay if you want," I said, but I didn't mean it, not quite.

"It's okay," he said.

When we were alone Stu sat down on the couch beside me and put his arm around my shoulders like he was the big brother.

"Did he tell you?" he asked.

"Tell me?"

"Whatever it was you needed to know."

"Yes," I said. "I guess so."

"I'll get the lights," said Stu, rising to his feet. As soon as it was dark I started to cry, like I'd only been waiting for the relief of being invisible. Stu was so quiet that I couldn't even tell where he was in the room. I'd never heard him be so silent. I quieted myself so that I could listen for him, to know if he was still there and then the room was cut in half by the beam of light from the slide projector. When I turned to look at the wall where the light was pointed I saw us all, big as life.

The picture was from the summer before the trip west. We were all on the front step of the house — our new home — and someone else was standing out on the street waiting to snap us all. I saw Hank with his arm large and protective as a wing draped over my mother's shoulder, and her smiling up into his face with a gaze that was, at that moment, clear and free of doubt. I saw Stu and me standing side by side with Mom's hand resting on his shoulder and Dad's resting on mine, so that we were all connected. I saw us all as if for the first time. I saw myself staring into the camera, confident that whatever was to come there would always be this moment when we were all together.

❧

There are things I said to my mother that I will never get the chance to take back.

When I was three my mother saved up to buy me a doll that she thought was very special, and on Christmas morning I saw her, the sweet blank-faced thing under the tree, and the first thing I did was to rip off all its clothes and turn it over so that I could see its back. I was looking for a pull string and when I didn't find one I threw her down. "She doesn't talk," I said. "I don't want her."

When I was five my mother and Hank sat me down and said that they'd decided to give me a little brother or sister. "Don't bother," I said. "I don't need one."

Once I said to her: "I don't think you ever put me first. I would have liked to be first in someone's life, if only once."

꒯

When my mother died she left me her fire safe. It is modern and anonymous looking and I keep it in my closet buried under a pile of old quilts. Some days I don't think of it at all. At other times I catch myself repeating the numbers of the combination, like the words to a song.

Stu offered to open the fire safe for me. He said that he could see what was inside and then either tell me or not tell me.

"Maybe it's empty," he said. "Or maybe her novel is in there."

"Or maybe the truth about me," I said.

I still haven't opened the fire safe. I don't know everything about myself or my mother, and the fire safe may hold the answers, but once opened it will be like the close of a conversation that I don't want to end. Not just yet.

❧

Stu has this song that he plays sometimes; he won't give it a name, because he says that it's really not a song at all. It changes a little every time he plays it, according to the weather on that day, the listeners present, and other factors too minute and particular to list. I call it the Memory Song. He played it at our mother's funeral. Part of the song is us in our car, the old green Volvo, on the highway. All of us together. Somewhere underneath that is the sound of Dad singing "Freedom's just another word" and the sound of our mother folding and re-folding her map, imagining towns where everybody had red hair, and Dad singing, "I'd trade all my tomorrows for a single yesterday," and myself, turning the pages of my book and sighing when my mother tried to get me to look at something outside the window, and the wheels turning and turning, and Stu recording it all, remembering everything by the vibrations in the air.

❧

My mother appears to me in my dreams and we talk. When this first started happening, the me in the dream would forget that my mother was dead and we'd spend our time talking about a new movie, or the cost of coffee, or why the leaves on my fig tree were turning yellow. I realized that to talk with my dead mother was something to be treasured, but still the absurd and banal dream conversations continued. Finally I hit on the idea of writing things down: things to tell her, questions to ask her. As soon as I knew what I wanted to ask her she stopped making appearances in my dreams.

ta

My first memory is of flying and of my mother holding me safe
to her body. Hers is the first face I ever saw.

Printed in September 1998 by

in Boucherville, Quebec